Downstate Illinois

by

Wesley Payton

This is a work of fiction. Names, characters, places, and incidents are either the product of the author's imagination or are used fictitiously, and any resemblance to actual persons living or dead, business establishments, events, or locales, is entirely coincidental.

Downstate Illinois

COPYRIGHT © 2021 by Wesley Payton

Cover Art by *Debbie Taylor*

The Wild Rose Press, Inc.
PO Box 708
Adams Basin, NY 14410-0708
Visit us at www.thewildrosepress.com

Publishing History
First Edition, 2021
Trade Paperback ISBN 978-1-5092-3587-2
Digital ISBN 978-1-5092-3588-9

Published in the United States of America

Holy hell, it's cold. It's a sunny afternoon, but the gusting winds have made my face numb, though not enough to keep me from feeling the water at the corner of my eyes freeze. Slim suggested we go ice fishing. I imagined a warm little shanty with comfortable seats. Instead we're sitting atop upturned buckets out in the open on a frozen, windswept lake. Man, that guy's a dimwit. If I ever write him as a character in one of my books, I'll have to change his nickname to Dim…besides, Slim reminds me of a Jim Croce song.

"I have to see a man about a horse," I say. "Where should I go?"

"You told me you used to go fishing with your granddaddy, so you know the drill, go anywhere you want…just don't piss in the ice hole."

"You're an ice hole. You mean I have to walk all the way back to the bank to find a tree to pee on?"

"You don't have to—just go over there." Slim vaguely points behind him. "Trust me, I won't look."

"But we're on a lake. I already feel stupid enough out here in the open with no fish to show for our efforts. What if somebody happens to be passing by?"

"Then they'll get a little show—probably very little…only partially on account of the cold."

"Is it cold?" I stomp away. "I hadn't noticed."

Dedication

For my family, both in the big city and the small town.

Part One

Chapter 1

Holy hell, it's hot. It's not even summer yet, and the sun went down over an hour ago, but the humidity is as thick as soup, so I'm sweating through the back of my shirt. I've come to this roadhouse to cool down and have a bite to eat. In the gravel parking lot, out front of the cinderblock tavern, stands a tall neon sign that's shaped like a cowboy boot. Inside the bright blue boot is a detached ear. My first thought is that the crimson color of the ear means it must've been severed in a bar fight, but I think it's meant to signify that this is a good place to hear scorching, boot-scootin' country music…or at least it used to be back when the sign was installed. As I understand it, this place was quite a honky-tonk in its heyday. Now it's just a convenient place to get a drink and some barbecue if you happen to be in the middle of nowhere.

I push through the double doors, feeling like a real cowboy, until several sturdy-looking men leaning against the bar turn and give me the same unfriendly look. I take a stool near the end of the bar away from the welcoming committee. For a Friday night, this place seems pretty empty…plenty of cowboy hats but no boot scooting. The jukebox is playing a Kid Rock song. I don't know if I'm too old for this place or too citified, but I definitely don't belong here, which I guess is why I came. I've lived in this small town for a month now and haven't seen much more of it than the Walmart and the Waffle House. I feel the need to soak up some of the local milieu and maybe sample this tavern's much ballyhooed barbecue pork.

"What do you want?" the burly bartender asks.

"A menu—"

"Kitchen's closed."

"—and a Scotch."

"We only serve whiskey and beer."

"Scotch is whisky," I protest, "and it's eight o'clock…how can the kitchen be closed already?"

"We only got American whiskey, and the kitchen shuts down early on slow nights."

"When's the last time you had a busy night?"

"It's been a while," the barkeep answers. "Let's just say the cook doesn't get a lot of overtime. Now what can I get you to drink?"

"What's the local whiskey of choice?"

"Jim or Jack."

"I'll have a Jack Daniel's on the rocks then."

"No can do…the ice machine is busted."

"Will it be fixed soon?" I ask.

"Doubt it…the repair guy's in prison."

"Probably better off there than here," I say under my breath. "So then what's the local beer of choice?"

"Bud or Miller Lite."

"Then I'll have a milieu light."

Not a great joke…maybe I won't include it in the book, if I ever decide to write about this place. The bartender gives me a funny look, reaches under the bar into the beer cooler, and pulls out a longneck of Miller

Lite without taking his eyes off me. He sets the bottle in front of me and takes a 50 caliber bullet from his back pocket. It looks like the sort of ammunition one might use to hunt woolly mammoths. The spent round has a notch carved in the bottom that the bartender uses to pry the cap off my bottle of beer.

"Much obliged," I say. The bartender returns to the busier part of the bar. I drink my beer and scan the large, open room—all the anticipated accoutrements: beer signs on the plywood walls and peanut shells on the concrete floors. I catch the eye of a woman a few stools down, or rather she sees me looking at her reflection in the mirror behind the bar as she's rolling her eyes at a tall man in a camouflage jacket who's attempting to pitch woo.

"You stand out in this place like a freshly washed truck in winter," the fellow says—not the worst line I've ever heard in a bar.

One of his buddies shouts for him from the pool table near the jukebox. "You're up, Slim."

"Excuse me, darling," Slim says, taking his leave. "Business before pleasure, but I'll be back."

"No need to hurry on my account," the woman replies.

"Seems like quite a Casanova," I say once I'm sure he's out of earshot.

"He's a good guy. I've known him since grade school…but when he gets a few beers in him, he'll flirt with anything that uses the ladies' room."

"I don't think I'd ever date anyone I went to grammar school with."

"Well, it's a small town…not exactly a target rich environment."

"I can't imagine what it must be like for everyone to know your business."

"You don't have to imagine it, Weston," she tells me. "You're living it."

"How did you—"

"Like I said, it's a small town…word gets around, and a big-city writer moving here makes for big news. My name is Rebecca, by the way, though most folks call me Becky. I live in the old farmhouse down by Stony Creek."

"Oh, that's near me. I live in the red house on—"

"I know…you live about a mile from me, which, in these parts, practically makes us next-door neighbors. That house used to belong to the Andrews family until the bank foreclosed on them."

"I'm sorry to hear that."

"It's not your fault…it's just the way it is." She seems anxious to change the subject. "So why'd you move down here? I hope not for the anonymity."

"Nah, I could find that anywhere. I moved here because this town is the two things a writer needs: cheap and quiet."

"Aside from the occasional tornado, this place is quiet all right, and if you have money, I guess it's pretty cheap too, but I thought you were supposed to be some kind of successful novelist with—wait, don't tell me…your spinster series."

"Successful in the sense that I earn a living, which in the writing world means I make about as much as your average plumber."

"Plumbers do okay, but around here it's the farmers who make the big money."

"I didn't realize farming was such a lucrative profession...don't they still do those Farm Aid concerts like every year?"

"Yeah," Rebecca answers. "I went to the first one over in Champaign when I was a little girl...hearing Willie Nelson sing 'On the Road Again' is one of my earliest memories. However, farming isn't really a profession like you said but more a way of life that you're born into, so sure...a lot of the family farmers around here are dirt poor, but some of them over the generations have accumulated enough acreage and hired enough hands to do real well for themselves, though it can be tricky to differentiate the rich ones from the poor ones—especially for an outsider. Do you want to know how you can tell them apart?"

"Sure, I like knowing things."

"Horses. These farmers are all wannabe cowboys when you get right down to it, so rich or poor they feel most comfortable wearing beat-up boots and broken-in jeans, and they all drive around in muddy pickup trucks, but the rich farmers own horses."

"Huh," I say, which is what I usually say when I don't know what to say next. "I wonder if somewhere in Texas there's a wealthy rancher who owns a stable full of tractors."

"Could be, though most farmers usually rent their heavy farming machinery, so they don't tend to get too attached to their tractors, but they all want to own a horse someday."

"Sounds like my friends in the city—can't tell the doctors from the teachers...they all wear sweatshirts and sneakers on the weekends, but the doctors own boats."

"Is this dude bothering you?" Slim returns, holding a pool cue menacingly.

"Though the term 'dude' may be deemed an insult," I say, "as it's thought to derive from the song "Yankee Doodle" that—as I'm sure you recall—makes reference to a macaroni, which itself was a pejorative term for the affected fops who often wore dandyish wigs in the Rococo style; however, 'dude' has also come to mean a city dweller unfamiliar with rural ways, as in a dude ranch where city slickers stay to learn about cowboy life, in which case the term is quite accurate, and I therefore take no umbrage at you referring to me as such."

"I don't give a rooster's nuts about your umbrage," Slim says.

"That I do take offense to. If not for me, then for all the nutless cocks in the world. It's a good thing you're so much bigger than me, or else I'd whip your ass."

"You ain't man enough to wipe my ass."

"Okay, boys," Rebecca says. "That's enough. There'll be no ass whipping or wiping tonight. Slim, thanks for checking in on me, but I'm having a nice conversation with this fella, so please go back to shooting pool."

"He ain't from around here," Slim sneers, "and I don't like strangers in my bar."

"For your information, uh, Slime, is it…I grew up in this state."

"You're from the city, and down here we don't consider that little corner of the state part of Illinois."

"And all this time I thought it was pronounced *Illinoise*. You ought to consider Chicago part of the state, since Cook County makes up less than two percent of Illinois's area but is home to half its population. It's what keeps you southern Illinois rednecks living in a blue state. Man, I bet that really sticks in your craw."

"Don't you even know your geography?" Slim asks. "This here is central Illinois. I'd be almost as embarrassed to be a southern Illinois hillbilly as I would to be a Shit-cago liberal."

"I'm a liberal in the sense that I think we all ought to do more to help poor people…not in the sense that I personally should do more to help poor people," I say, attempting to introduce a bit of levity into this exchange. "I suppose your philosophy is teach a man to fish and he'll eat for a lifetime. That only works if you happen to live next to a fishing hole."

"Yep, I believe that folks need to do for themselves, and if I ain't much mistaken, Chicago is right next to a fairly sizeable lake. But all this talk of politics is—how would you college types put it—academic down here." Slim eyes my white hair. "Voting's only good for giving old people something to do, and speakin' of which, ain't you seen a few too many winters to be chatting up this young gal?"

"I'm not propositioning her. As she said, we're just having a nice conversation."

"Well, I don't like it, and I don't like you."

"So you've told me—strangers in your bar and all that. I imagine you've been coming here a long time. I'll make you a wager. If I can tell you something about this tavern that you don't know, will you agree to stop bothering me?"

"And if you can't?" Slim asks.

"Then I'll go."

"All right then."

"What's the name of this tavern?" I ask.

"This tavern ain't got no name…everybody knows that."

"Come on—you're not thinking it through. There may not be a name emblazoned on that sign out front, but this bar has to have a name to put on the deed or to be invoiced for alcohol for that matter."

"I…don't know what this bar's name is," Slim stammers.

"Again, you just need to think it through. Let me ask you another question: what's on that neon sign?"

"A boot…and an ear."

"There you have it," I say. "Boot and ear…it's a visual pun. The name of this bar is the Boutonniere, which happens to be French for buttonhole. I guess the original owners figured giving this place a French name hidden within a rebus would make it a little classier, though I suspect they hadn't counted on your future patronage."

"There's no way this place is called The Boutonniere." Slim seethes. "You're talking out of your buttonhole, and I want you to zip it."

"You want me to zip my buttonhole…impossible."

"He's right, Slim," says the bartender, who began hovering nearby when he saw the tall man approach with a pool stick. "When they first opened this place way back when, it was known as the Boutonniere, but then my daddy bought it even though he thought the name was too fruity, and he always overcharged anybody who said it, so nobody calls it that anymore."

"I'll be damned," Slim says. "I've been coming to this place for most of my life, and I didn't know all that."

"Barkeep," I say, "I'd like to order another round for me, my new friend Slim, and the lovely Rebecca."

"I'm a man of my word," says Slim, "so you can stay, but we ain't friends yet, and I only let my friends buy me beer."

Slim goes back to shooting pool, while Rebecca and I drink our drinks and continue our conversation.

"That was pretty clever the way you figured out the name of this place from the sign out front," she tells me. "I've been coming here almost as long as Slim, and I didn't know this bar had a name either."

"I must confess it wasn't all that clever. The other reason I moved here is because I used to have family that lived in this town...a grandfather who has long since passed. He'd tell me stories about this place in its salad days."

"Were you two close?"

"He died when I was fifteen, but yeah...he meant a lot to me. I'd spend summers down here with him."

"That must've been nice," Rebecca says wistfully, her voice starting to sound drowsy.

"It was...now I don't have family anywhere. Chicago's great, but it's a big city, and cities are always changing...it's the small towns that tend to stay the same. The house I bought—that the Andrews lived in—was built by my granddad...that's where I stayed when I visited. My father sold it when he passed...not to the Andrews. I don't know how many owners that house has had since Granddad died, but I'm at a point in my life when I want to put down roots someplace that feels familiar, so when I found out the old house was up for sale, I figured it would be as good a place as any."

"Most people don't usually have many nice things to say about living here, but really it's not such a bad place to be."

"Did you ever think about leaving?"

"I did leave...for a while, but it didn't stick. Something kept calling me back. Listen to me...I'm starting to sound nostalgic like somebody going through a midlife crisis. Sorry, I didn't mean to suggest that you're in crisis...or middle-aged."

"Well, I'm fifty-one, so if that makes me middle aged, then it must mean I'll live to be 102, which doesn't sound so bad."

"I would've put you in your mid-forties...maybe just ten years older than me. Sorry again, I tend to think out loud when I get a little tipsy. I didn't mean to stay so long, but I can't remember the last time I've had such a pleasant conversation. Anyway, I should go."

"Can I call you a cab?"

"There're no cabs to call out here. Used to be that the cops didn't care if you drove home after one too many drinks...there's hardly anyone else on the roads to crash into, except the odd deer or maybe a cornfield, but with all the foreclosures lately, the township has lost a lot of revenue in property taxes, so they've found a new revenue stream with DUIs."

"I got a later start here than you," I say. "Why don't you let me drive you home?"

"I may be younger than you, but I'm not that young."

"I promise to be a perfect gentleman." In this dark bar, her eyes are luminous. What is it with her eyes? I usually only find the parts of a woman that are unique to their fairer sex alluring—everybody's got eyes…though not like hers.

"I can tell you're a gentleman, but I don't expect you to be too perfect." She blushes and then giggles. "I really must be tipsy. I've only ever picked up a guy in a bar once before, and I swore I'd never do it again. I don't want you thinking I'm some sort of ho wagon."

"No, of course not…I don't think you're any kind of wagon." Maybe the beers I drank on an empty stomach have gone to my head too. "So what happened last time…you know, when you picked up a guy in a bar?"

"We got divorced after twelve years of marriage and two kids."

"Ah…that can sometimes happen."

"Still want to drive me home?"

"Sure," I say with a wink, "I was ready to leave anyway." I can't remember the last time I actually winked at a woman…she makes me feel foolish and confident all at the same time.

"Before we go," she whispers as she puts her hand on my knee under the bar, "I want you to describe your lovemaking prowess in a single word."

"Brobdingnagian."

"What does that even mean?" she asks with another giggle.

"I don't remember…it was just the biggest word I could think of. I'd tell you more about my lovemaking prowess, but I'm afraid modesty forbids it."

"Then maybe I'll just have to judge for myself."

Chapter 2

I awaken to birds chirping and the morning sun casting shadows from the tree branches just outside the window. I still haven't gotten used to waking up in my new house rather than my old tenth-floor apartment. Wait...my bedroom doesn't have tree limbs outside the window. My house is a single-story ranch. I turn over in bed and see Rebecca waking up too. She smiles at me. We hear the doorbell downstairs. Her smile disappears.

"Oh shit." She sits straight up. I guess this day isn't going to start the way I'd hoped.

"Are you expecting visitors?"

"No...my kids." She jumps out of bed and into a pair of jeans. "My sister is dropping off the boys...I guess I forgot to set the alarm last night."

"You were a little distracted."

"Hey, listen." She frantically pulls on a sweatshirt. "I really like you, and I hope to see you again, but you've got to go. It'd be weird for my boys to know a man stayed over. How do you feel about leaving through the window?"

"But we're on the second floor."

"There's a sturdy tree limb that almost touches the window. The trunk is pretty far from the house, but I think you could make it."

"The heart's willing, but the fall would probably cause my knees to crumble."

"So last night must've made you weak in the knees." She pulls her hair into a ponytail.

"Last night and the fifty years before that," I begin to say, "but mostly last night."

I get out of bed and pull on my pants. As I'm searching for my shirt, a woman who looks remarkably like Rebecca knocks on the bedroom door as she slowly pushes it open.

"Becky, did you trade in your Jeep? That car in the driveway is fancy, but it looks like it might have a lot of mileage. Did you end up going out after your meeting? I'm glad you had a chance to sleep in, but I'm running late for my shift, so—" She notices me just as I find my shirt hanging from the bedpost. "Oh...I didn't realize you had company."

"Kim, this isn't what you think."

"There's a half-naked man in your bedroom." Kim looks me up and down, lingering on my white hair. "What am I supposed to think...that Santa Claus came early?"

"Auntie, did you say Santa Claus?" a kid's voice asks from the stairs.

"Thanks, sis," Rebecca says as the boy tries to peek in from the hallway.

"Sorry," Kim replies, "this whole situation just caught me a little by surprise. I mean, I'm glad that you're dating again, but—"

"Is mommy dating Santa Claus?" The boy wiggles past Kim into the bedroom.

"I'm not Santa Claus," I say, pulling on my shirt, "but I get that a lot because of my white hair, though as you can see...no beard."

"Then who are you?" he asks.

"Well...I'm a friend of your mother's." I extend my hand. "My name is Weston Payley. What's your name?"

The boy cautiously shakes my hand. "My name is Lance...Lance Delacroix...or is it Lance Hernandez now, Mommy?"

"Sweetie, remember, I changed my last name back to...well, my last name, but your name is still Delacroix—like your daddy's."

"So Daddy left our home but kept his name," the boy says as if trying to understand a difficult arithmetic problem, "and you stayed here with us but changed your name...and now a guy who looks like a skinny Santa Claus sleeps in Daddy's old room with you?"

"Oh god." Rebecca puts one hand on her forehead and the other on her son's shoulder. "Weston, Lance is my youngest boy."

"I just turned nine."

"That's right, sweetie." She directs Lance back into the hallway. "Why don't we all go downstairs? I'll introduce you to my oldest son, Vance."

"He's almost sixteen," Lance informs me as I enter the hallway, "and he prefers to be called Van."

"So you're Weston Payley, the romance writer." Kim follows me into the hallway. "The whole town has been talking about you."

"Oh god," Rebecca says again from the stairs in front of me. We descend into the living room. Vance is sitting on the couch next to where one of my shoes landed. I can tell from the glare he gives me that for him the arithmetic was pretty easy.

"Vancy," Rebecca says timorously, "I'd like you to meet a friend of mine—"

"I heard." Van stands up. "Like Santa Claus but not Santa Claus. What'd he do, come down your chimney last night to give you his package?"

"That's enough, Vance," Kim says curtly.

"Did you lick his candy cane?"

"Vancy, please don't do this," Rebecca pleads. "I've been divorced from your father for over two years."

"Yeah"—Van storms toward the front door—"and now you've replaced him with Mr. Romance Writer. By the way, little brother, it's time you learned there's no such thing as Santa Claus."

Vance slams the door behind him. During the silent moment that follows, Rebecca, Kim, and Lance all turn to look at me. "Often people mistake my books for romance novels because they each have the word spinster in the title, but I think of them more as adventure stories."

"Oh god," Rebecca says for the third time.

Chapter 3

I sit alone, waiting in a corner booth of what is likely this town's fanciest restaurant...a pizza parlor. Rebecca had called earlier today, both to thank me for the ride home on Friday night and to apologize for the abrupt awakening yesterday morning. I told her that no thanks or apologies were necessary, but I asked if she wanted to have dinner some night. She answered that she was free this evening, which I'd hoped was why she'd called, but that her sister could only watch the kids until nine o'clock, so there wouldn't be any time for dessert.

I've been sipping a glass of the house red for the last twenty minutes. I can't tell if the wine is closer to a cabernet or a pinot noir, but it tastes fine, albeit in a nondescript sort of way...it's the waiting that's leaving a bad taste in my mouth. As I swallow the last of my wine, I consider leaving a twenty-dollar bill on the table and heading for the door when I see Rebecca walk in. She looks as lovely as the last time I saw her, but more dressed up. She's traded her jeans for a dress...but not some meretricious cocktail dress—just a nice dress. Yes, she looks lovely in her nice dress. Not the most poetic way this lonely writer has ever described a woman, but apt. She walks toward me and manages to class up this pizza joint along the way.

"Sorry I'm late," she says, sliding into the booth.

"You don't have to apologize for anything looking the way you do."

"Ah, flattery, I like that."

"I was going to tell you that you stand out like a freshly washed truck in winter, but I didn't want to sound unoriginal."

"Honestly, that wasn't the worst line I've ever heard at that bar."

"It's certainly memorable."

"So what were you drinking?"

"Wine," I answer, "red...I'm afraid that's as specific as I can be. Can I order you a glass? I'd offer to split a bottle with you, but I think they might bring us a jug instead."

"They get their wines in boxes, so let's split a carafe."

"Sounds good." I signal for the waitress. "You know this place...what's good here?"

"The garbage pizza is excellent," she tells me with a straight face.

"Yeah...that sounds appetizing."

"Hey, Becky," the waitress says as she approaches our table. "What can I get for you two?"

"We'll have a carafe of the house red," I order, "and a large, deep-dish garbage pizza."

"Sorry," the waitress says, "we don't have thick crust."

"Sure...thin crust sounds good too."

"Sorry again, we just have our regular crust."

"That'll be fine...please tell Ramone I said 'hey.' " Rebecca turns to me. "I promise you'll love it."

With that the waitress heads back toward the kitchen.

"Is Ramone her husband?"

"No, he's the guy who makes the pizzas," she tells me. "He knows I like extra spinach."

"You've really got this town wired."

"You don't live someplace most of your life without learning a few things."

"I don't know, I lived most of my life in the same city thinking there were just two kinds of pizza crust."

"Right, paper thin or phonebook thick...somehow Chicago manages to exist in Middle America without really being in the middle."

"It hasn't got much of a middle class," I say, "at least not in the city proper—you're either rich or poor."

"You're automatically considered middle class in this town if you have a job."

"What's your job?"

"Oh," she says with a gleam in her eye, "a first-date question."

"You already know what I do, but I'd like to know what you do."

"Take a guess."

"Mayor."

"No, but I went to homecoming with his younger brother...the McCormick family are nice people."

"Beautician."

"I think they prefer to be called cosmetologists these days."

"Teacher."

"Close," she says. "I'm a social worker. Mostly I work with young people struggling with addiction."

"Who works with the older people?"

"No one, they usually won't get help unless it's court ordered, and even then, more often than not, they end up back in prison rather than going to counseling."

"So what's the drug du jour these days?"

"Well, it was meth, but like everywhere else, we've got an opioid epidemic on our hands…and still meth. For most of the addicts I work with, opioids are the ones they need, and meth is the one they want. Usually, before I get to them, they've found a way to help themselves to a good deal of both."

"Sounds challenging."

"It keeps me busy, but there's a work farm that opened up not too far from here a while back that seems to be helping a lot of people."

"Maybe they'll put you out of business."

"Nothing would make me happier," she says with a sigh.

"And yet you said 'seems to be helping.' "

"I don't know…just a hunch or a bad vibe. My small, underfunded agency is in the same business as the Big Farm, as it's called, but every time we reach out to them to follow up on a former client now under their care, we get stonewalled. There's been absolutely no information reciprocity or even professional courtesy for that matter, and they appear to be operating with effectively no government oversight…but then maybe I'm just disappointed that they seem to be succeeding where I've failed."

"You don't strike me as the kind of person who fails all that often," I say, "and when you do, as everyone does, I suspect you're the type who learns from it."

"Thanks, but I'm aware I have a chip on my shoulder about this. I left college when I found out I was pregnant with Vance; his father and I got married soon after. I looked after Vance, and Rod worked construction. He had a fall at a work site and suffered a spinal fracture. Turns out when he was injured, he had a BAC over the legal limit to drive—my ex never was much of an abstainer…of anything—so the construction company was off the hook for most of the worker's comp beyond the initial medical bills. Of course, they didn't want anything further to do with him once he was better. So I went back to school to finish my degree and became a social worker with a certification in drug counseling…all while my husband's oxycodone prescription for his lingering back pain progressed into a full-blown heroin addiction. Mind you, this happened right under my nose, and I never noticed until I had to miss my graduation because he was in the hospital recovering from an overdose."

"That's a kick in the gut all right…still, from what I understand, it can happen to anyone."

"I'm a drug counselor," Rebecca says defensively, "I know addiction can happen to anyone."

"No, I mean living with an addict and not knowing it."

"Oh…yeah, I've seen plenty of that too…sorry."

"You don't need to be sorry…and you also don't need to be so hard on yourself."

"I hear you, it's just difficult, you know. I thought we'd turned a corner when we had Lance—things seemed to be going well for us…and then they weren't. It was off and on like that for years until finally I cut him loose. Now he pops up at the most unexpected times. I occasionally see his name on paperwork that comes through my office...or on a first date at a pizza parlor."

"Yikes—that sounds awkward." I follow her eyes to the pick-up window in the restaurant's lobby. "Oh, is that him?"

"Yeah," she almost whispers, "but he probably won't see us all the way back here."

"Okay, Becky, here's your carafe of wine," the waitress cheerfully announces as she approaches our table.

It's enough. Rod turns his head and spots Rebecca and me. He walks toward us, carrying two take-out pizzas.

"Oh god," Rebecca says under her breath.

"Well, hell's bells," Rod says as he takes the place of the retreating waitress. "It's my ex-wife out on the town...and who might you be?"

"I might be any number of people," I say, "but as it happens my name is Weston."

"Ah, the romance writer...I've heard about you."

"I like to think of myself as more of an adventure writer."

"Either way, my name's Rodney, and I'm damn glad to meet you." He sticks out his fist and points it in my direction.

"I'm not sure what's happening," I say. "Are we dueling?"

"No, man," he says with a grin, "I'm trying to give you a fist bump."

"Oh, I get it." I partially stand and bump my fist against his. "I'm not accustomed to fist-bumping, though I did see Barrack Obama do it once, but I've sworn off trying to be cool ever since the backward baseball cap fizzled out."

"Hey," he says, "a backward cap keeps the back of your neck from getting sunburnt."

"Since when do you go by Rodney?" Rebecca asks.

"Believe it or not, I've matured some since the last time you saw me."

"Your eyes certainly look clearer," she says.

"I've been clean and sober for months now." Rodney seems pleased with himself and embarrassed all at the same time.

"It must agree with you...I see you've lost some weight," she observes. "What have you been doing with yourself?"

"I've been working out at the Big Farm. They work us from sunup to sundown and then some—eighty hours a week...no time left in the day for any foolishness."

"That's a lot of hours," Rebecca says.

"We work six twelve-hour days a week and then just eight hours on Sunday, so tonight is sort of our night off. The work is hard, but I like it."

"Must be good money with all that overtime pay," I offer.

"It's farm work so they don't pay overtime, but...yeah, it adds up when you ain't got no time to spend it and no habit to feed. In fact, Becky, I should be able to pay you that child support I owe you real soon."

"That would be helpful," Rebecca replies.

"Anyways, I got some people waiting for me out in the truck, so I'll let you get back to your dinner, but it was good seeing you again and nice to meet you."

"Take care of yourself," she says as he turns to leave. Rebecca watches him with an open mouth as he exits the restaurant. "Wow!"

"I thought he seemed like a nice guy."

"I know...wow." She shakes her head in disbelief. "He's like a completely different person."

"I take it he hasn't always been such a nice guy?"

"It depends on who you ask."

"I'm asking you."

"He's always been protective...bordering on possessive. When we first started dating, this guy I only went out with a couple of times told Rod...Rodney that he was lucky to be seeing me. He took the comment the wrong way and got into a fight with the guy."

"Did he beat him up pretty bad?"

"No, the guy had played center on the high school football team...big fella. I think he's a Marine now. Anyway, Rodney got his nose broken and a tooth knocked out."

I fill our wine glasses. "Sounds like he learned a lesson."

"Rod's never been much of a learner. A month later, he sees the guy in a bar and follows him into the restroom...with a hand grenade. I have no idea how he got it, but I know the story's true because they weren't the only two people in the restroom."

"So what happened?"

"Rod blocked the door and handed the guy the grenade...without the pin in it. Rod told the guy that if he ever mentioned my name again, the last thing he'd see would be that grenade. The guy gave the grenade back and enlisted in the military that same week."

"That's quite a story." I set my wine glass on the table. "Makes me never want to use a public restroom again. You don't think he still has that grenade, do you?"

"No, he and some of his drinking buddies used it to blow up an old car on the Fourth of July later that summer."

"Rodney seems like he has a real special way of doing things."

"Rod was special all right, but I understood him—mostly, but the Rodney you just met...I don't understand him at all."

"Maybe he finally learned how to be a learner...maybe the Big Farm has really done him some good."

"Maybe...I hope so. I can't stand my ex, but I still care about him—you know?"

"Not really," I answer, "I've never been married."

"Is that right? I half thought the reason you moved here was because you just went through something like a messy divorce...not that any of them are ever clean."

"Nope, I never married...thought about it a couple of times. I liked the idea of having someone around but couldn't abide the idea of having someone around all the damn time. It's funny, in the city I lived alone, but everywhere I went I was surrounded by people, so I felt the opposite of lonely. Here though...I don't know, perhaps it's the crickets or the corn or you...I have—oh, I'll say it in the local patois—a hankering for companionship."

"So you're saying I'm on par with corn and crickets then?"

"Well, corn is sweet and crickets are cute, so I guess I am."

"Are there any more like you where you come from?"

"Bunches….too many, in fact. I had to move here just so I could be unique."

Rebecca smiles at me with her eyes, but before she can say anything, the waitress arrives with our pizza. It smells delectable.

Chapter 4

Walmart is like the watering hole of this small-town habitat—the common ground. I've met enough of the locals in the short time that I've been seeing Rebecca that I try to go early in the morning to this twenty-four-hour general store to buy my groceries and cleaning supplies so as to avoid those endless conversations in the aisles, during which your ice cream melts and you feel embarrassed about the liquor in your cart.

I'm perusing the mops when I see a man walk past my aisle wearing an Apple Watch on one wrist and a Patek Philippe on the other. As I consider how odd it is that someone wearing either of those two timepieces would be in Walmart at this hour, the man walks back into frame at the end of the aisle, completing the most dramatic of double takes.

"Weston…is that you?"

"Never heard of him." I put the steam mop I was examining back on the shelf. "It's good to see you again, Geoff."

"Likewise." Geoff extends his Apple hand for me to shake. "What in the world are you doing down here?"

"Just mopping around mostly." We execute a halfhearted handshake. "I have a house here that has good bones but needs a lot of TLC."

"You still have your place up in the city though, don't you?"

"No, I got rid of it. I'm a local yokel these days."

He purses his lips in reflexive condescension. "I imagine these quiet surroundings afford you an opportunity to write with very few distractions."

Ugh, the rich. They think anyone who doesn't own at least two homes is impecunious. I met smug Geoff years ago during the Venetian Nights boat festival back in Chicago when he was showing off his new sailing yacht to a woman I was dating. I think he befriended me just so that he could tell people he knew a writer—to round out his collection of friends—and so he could spend more time with my then girlfriend. He threw good parties though.

"So what are you doing at a Walmart in downstate Illinois at 6:30 in the morning?" I ask.

"Is it as early as that?"

"A man who wears two watches doesn't know the time?"

"Oh," Geoff says with a slight reddening of his face, as if noticing for the first time that he has a watch on each wrist, which is the closest approximation of humility that I've ever seen him evince. "I fly down a couple of times a year to spend a few days at a shooting ranch not too far from here. We mostly hunt deer and waterfowl when they're in season, but the property has a range too."

"Sounds rustic."

"I suppose it's rustic without the roughing it bit...sort of like glamping. Anyway, one of my domestic employees packed my travel bag, and I just realized that he only packed dress socks, so I had the airport's shuttle stop here so I could purchase some insulated socks, but—as I'm sure you're aware—it's a tiny airport that likely doesn't pay its drivers very well, so I thought it best to remove the formal watch that my domestic packed as my bag is now unattended with the driver. As for the Apple watch…I'd be lost without regular updates from my offices."

"I've noticed that cell service can be pretty spotty outside of town."

"The compound has Wi-Fi," Geoff informs me. "Hey, why don't you drop by tonight? They're having something of a soiree this evening. I'll have to give you directions as it's a little tricky to find; the entrance is on an unmarked road."

"Uh…sure, why not. Should I bring a date?"

"Gentlemen only, I'm afraid, but do bring that bottle of blended Scotch in your cart. I imagine some of the older members will be amused by it."

Chapter 5

I've been driving backroads for half an hour, and it'll be dark soon. If I don't find this place in a hurry, I'll have to suspend my search. The last landmark Geoff mentioned was a mud puddle. How can a puddle be a landmark? The wheels of my car bounce along a bumpy road that's more dirt than gravel. Then suddenly my car splashes into almost a foot of water. Ah…more of a pond than a puddle, but at least I've found it. I drive through the muddy water, hoping my car can take it, and hook a hard right onto a grassy lane that runs along a barbed wire fence. A canopy of trees obscures the last of the setting sun. Before long the lane leads me to an enormous open area. My grateful tires and spine feel smooth pavement once again. The grounds look as manicured as a golf course. I drive up to an imposing gate. A guard leans out the window of the gatehouse.

"Can I help you?"

"I'm here for the soiree…I'm a friend of Geoff's."

"Right, he phoned earlier about a guest for this evening." The guard consults his clipboard. "Your name is Wesley Payton, I presume?"

"Close…Weston Payley." The security measures here are impressive. The compound is well cloistered and the guard courteous but cunning.

"My mistake, Mr. Payley." The guard gives me a knowing nod as he presses the button to raise the gate.

"I'm currently reading John Grisham's *The Appeal*, and I confused your name with one of his characters."

"No problem at all." Security guards with a concealed carry permit and a gym membership are easy enough to come by, but guards that actually read are scarce and, from what I understand, pricey. "That's quite a puddle back there."

"Yes, it's a chore to keep filled when we get into the dry part of summer. Drive up to the main house…you can't miss it. A valet will park your car, and someone will be waiting to show you to the drawing room."

I drive through the open gate and continue along the winding road. I soon see a mansion on a hill in the distance. I pass various outbuildings and finally pull up to the front entrance, coming to a stop under the porte cochère. A uniformed man comes over from the valet stand and opens my door for me. As the valet drives off with my car to who knows where, another man in a more ostentatious uniform descends the stairs and beckons for me to follow him. He leads me through the foyer and down a long hall. On the walls hang old oil paintings depicting various hunting tableaus and the mounted heads of well-antlered deer. I find their glassy-eyed stares disquieting, as if they're considering how a taxidermic trophy of my head might look up on the wall with them.

"Sir, we have arrived at the drawing room." The butler-type person opens the door for me to enter. I consider tipping him, but his haughty demeanor makes me think he probably has more money in the bank than I do.

The room is as big as a gymnasium. Leather chairs are arranged around an immense stone fireplace. A large billiards table occupies the center of the room. Along the back wall stands an antique-looking bar constructed of dark woods with intricate inlays. "If this is the drawing room, then where are all the easels?"

"Congratulations, sir, that's as close as I've ever heard anyone get to successfully executing that particular witticism. I believe you will find your friend at the bar."

The butler closes the door behind me, and I cross the room toward the booze. Geoff spots me in the bar's mirror as I make my way past the billiards table.

"Weston, my good man, so nice of you to stop by." Geoff's greeting is too vociferous for this cavernous but quiet room. I notice a few heads turn, as if irritated that the crackling of the fire has been interrupted.

"This is a nice place," I say just loud enough for him to hear me as I approach the bar, hoping that he'll match my volume. "Thanks for inviting me."

"Of course—you are quite welcome." No such luck with the volume control. "Now what can we get you to drink?"

"I brought this." I give him the frugal bottle of multi-malt Scotch that he had asked me to bring this morning.

"Oh…I meant that as a joke." Geoff accepts the bottle and then hands it off to the bartender. "Barkeep, let's put this below the bar, and we'll have two glasses of that single malt Scotch I've been drinking."

"Yes, sir," says the bartender as he puts my bottle out of sight and then pulls a bottle whose label I don't recognize off the top shelf behind him. He pours two glasses neat and sets them in front of us.

Geoff holds up his glass for us to clink together. I already regret coming. We make the stupid clinking sound with our glasses and then sip our damn Scotch. "Peaty."

"Very," Geoff replies, as if sipping bog water was the best thing in the world. "Let me introduce you to some of the members." Geoff scans the room. At the other end of the otherwise unoccupied bar sits an old man with his head resting on a coaster; I'm not sure if he's asleep or dead. Geoff motions for the bartender and then points to the old man. "Maybe he's had enough. Perhaps you should call a couple of the staff to help him to his room."

"Right away, sir." The bartender pulls a cordless phone from under the bar and presses a single button.

"Come, I'll introduce you to Dr. Weize. He's a psychology professor at the university, and one of our most prominent members. I know he's still awake...I've been told that he hardly ever sleeps."

"Is bedtime always so early here?" We pass a few other men snoozing in wingback chairs. "Certainly the flickering fire, the dark room, and the aged whisky must have a somnolent effect, but it's not even nine o'clock yet."

"Some of our members are quite elderly, and a lot of our younger members come down here to take a respite from their hectic careers—many of them are doctors—so they're more interested in rest than recreation. Factor in that the hunting usually starts early in the morning, and the cocktails start flowing early in the evening…well, we don't have a lot of late nights here."

Geoff leads me to a small table where a man about our age sits alone, flipping through a binder with glassine pages containing rows of stamps.

"Professor," Geoff says, announcing our presence. "I'd like to introduce you to a friend of mine, Weston Payley."

The professor turns slowly away from his stamps to look at the two of us. His mouth, with some effort, forms the shape of a smile.

"A pleasure to make your acquaintance, Mr. Payley," the professor says as he partially stands, making a small bow, and then quickly retakes his seat. "Your name sounds familiar to me."

"I thought it might," Geoff says before I can respond. "Weston is a writer, and since philology is a hobby of yours—"

"It appears Dr. Weize's hobby is philately," I correct.

"Quite so," says the professor, "but language is also of interest to me, as it should be for anyone who utilizes it. After all, language is mankind's greatest invention. What is it that you write, Mr. Payley?"

"Adventure books," I answer.

"I think most people think of them more as romance novels," Geoff adds, "though from what I hear, they're real page turners."

"Right," the professor says slowly, as if tuning in an image on an old television set, "you're that spinster fellow."

"That's correct," I say, "and you're a psych prof?"

"Yes, I'm a professor of psychological sciences at the university, but I've been on sabbatical for the last year pursuing another project."

"The doc lends a hand over at the Big Farm," Geoff informs. "It's a work farm that helps addicts get clean."

"I'm familiar with it. A woman I met recently is a social worker and has mentioned it to me. She tells me that your farm seems to be helping a number of people."

"We do what we can," Dr. Weize says, sounding both humble and arrogant.

"But how do you do it?" I ask. "You appear to have some sort of magic formula that no one else has discovered."

"I employ some rather progressive addiction treatment techniques that have proven successful."

"Like what? Surely you wouldn't want to keep the reason for your success a secret."

"Of course not," the professor replies with an air of indignation. "After all, my work is pro bono. I intend to publish a paper very soon outlining my techniques."

"Care to outline them now?" I ask. "You know, in broad strokes for a layperson like me."

"Psychoanalytic therapy is at the core of my program—associative memory, operant conditioning …that sort of thing."

"But what does that sort of thing entail exactly…in a nutshell?"

"In a nutshell, I explore childhood memories in therapy, cherry-pick the useful ones, and disregard the rest."

"Cherry-pick the useful ones in order to make your patients happier?"

"Happiness?" Dr. Weize asks rhetorically. "I could accomplish that faster and easier with drugs...at least for a little while, and not because the drugs lose efficacy but because the human mind isn't wired for interminable happiness...that's the stuff of fairy tales, I'm afraid. Everlasting happiness just isn't viable, evolutionarily speaking; it would result in indolence and atrophy. The mind has an innate desire for happiness, but no long-term capacity for it. My program doesn't make my patients feel better; it simply makes them better people. Every patient has trauma in their past. Certainly a war orphan has experienced different trauma than someone who grew up in an affluent suburb, but I can use what's there just the same...everything I require is available in aggregate. I associate a patient's childhood trauma with their negative impulses and voila...the result is an adult who's now content to be a productive member of society."

"That sounds a little like brainwashing," I accuse.

"It might sound that way, as you said, to a layperson such as yourself, but I assure you that my techniques conform to the strict guidelines established by the APA's Board of Social and Ethical Responsibility for Psychology." Dr. Weize somehow manages to look down his nose at me while staring up at us from his seated position. "But let's not forget that these are desperate people on paths toward self-destruction, and sometimes desperate people require desperate measures, so I think you'll agree that washing the brain of defects—to borrow your colloquialism—is the lesser of two evils."

"Makes sense to me," says Geoff the genius. "If it keeps the addicts off the streets, then I'm all for it."

"So Mr. Payley," Dr. Weize says, seeming eager to segue to another topic of conversation, "are you considering membership in our little club?"

"Not Weston." Geoff slaps me on the back for some reason. "He's too much of a lefty to join a gun club."

"I don't consider myself to be a political man," Dr. Weize says, "but if I were, I'd likely be a liberal too, and I'm a vegetarian, so I don't hunt; however, I do very much enjoy the precision of target shooting. Perhaps you'll join us at the range someday soon to try the sport of shooting for yourself."

"Do you shoot those clay pigeons here?" I ask. "I've never fired a gun in my life, but I've always wanted to try that."

"Of course," answers Geoff, slapping me on the back again. "We've got a great skeet shooting range. Why don't you come back tomorrow and give it a shot?"

"I prefer pistols and rifles myself," Dr. Weize adds, "but I'd be glad to shoot shotguns with you two tomorrow."

Chapter 6

I've been seeing quite a bit of Rebecca these last few weeks, though, if I'm being honest with myself, I wouldn't mind seeing even more of her. Most days I feel like I'm biding my time, occupying myself with purposeless errands and chores, waiting until our next date. I moved here for the peace and quiet; now I have dumpster loads of both, but my writing has gone all to hell. There doesn't seem to be any conflict in the world anymore…at least none that couldn't be solved with an open line of communication and a willingness to work things out—not the best mindset for a professional storyteller.

I'm waiting to meet her for lunch at her favorite Mexican restaurant—the Salsa Cauldron. She says it's the best of the three taquerias that have opened in the area over the last couple of years. Before then, as I understand it, the town's most ethnic food was pizza. It's a good place to get a quick bite, as she usually doesn't have much time for lunch. Today we might have even less time, since she's running about twenty minutes late, and I'm due out at the shooting ranch soon.

I glance up from my table as I hear someone come through the door. It's not Rebecca, but rather a tall man in a police uniform. He looks familiar to me, and I notice an expression of recognition on his face as we make eye contact. He crosses the small restaurant and stands next to my table, sneering down at me.

"Slime," I say, "is that a bellhop's outfit you're wearing?"

"Nope," Slim answers, "it's my police officer's uniform."

"What's that make you then—one of the Village People? I would've figured you more for the village idiot."

"What it makes me is an officer of the law…as in you do what I tell you and you won't go to jail. Don't do what I tell you, and—"

"I will…I get it. So what is it that you want, Constable Slime?"

"Your presence has been requested at the mayor's office."

"How about after lunch? I'm meeting someone."

"Becky's waiting with Mayor McCormick now."

"Is everything okay?"

"No." Slim's face turns serious. "But Becky's fine."

"Then what's the problem?"

"The problem is you're asking too many damn questions. Get your ass up and into my squad car, or I'll arrest you."

"For what?"

"Resisting arrest—that one's my personal favorite."

"You can't arrest me for resisting arrest—that'd be like giving someone a speeding ticket before they start their car."

"You'd think so, but you'd be wrong."

Chapter 7

Officer Slim escorts me into the mayor's office, which is located in a strip mall whose anchor store is a 7-Eleven. As we enter, Rebecca gives me a frowny smile from one of the chairs set in front of a large antique desk that looks about as out of place as vegetables in a convenience store. The man behind the desk, mumbling into a phone, must be the mayor.

"Got to go." He hangs up the phone and eyes me as I sit in the empty chair next to Rebecca, leaving Slim to hover in the background. "Thanks for coming."

"I didn't have much of a choice."

The mayor seems irritated, and then—like all politicians do when they become aware that they're manifesting signs of irritation—he lets out a blithe but insincere chuckle. "Sorry about that. I instructed the good officer to inform you that your presence was merely a request."

"He did, and then the huckleberry threatened to cuff me if I didn't comply. So what's this all about?"

"Forgive the state of my temporary office." The mayor rises from his desk and moves toward the storefront window to—I guess—survey the parking lot. "The municipal building downtown, where my office is usually located, is being renovated. You may not know this, but it was built before the Civil War...beautiful old building, though it was in desperate need of a new roof.

We had to pass a referendum to fund its repair and get the building up to code."

"I suppose I should've known better than to ask an elected official a direct question." I stand from my chair. "Take care now." Slim moves to block my exit. Rebecca grabs my hand without rising to leave with me.

"Please, sit down—won't you?" The mayor returns to his desk. "I apologize...this is difficult for me to talk about. My son died several days ago in a farming accident."

I retake my seat. "I'm sorry."

"Thank you—as you can imagine, it's been a trying time for his mother and me. He was a good kid—graduated high school last year...played on the baseball team, but unfortunately he'd lost his way since then."

"I'd worked with him off and on for a few months a while back," Rebecca says—about time she spoke up. "He'd gotten into trouble with drugs—"

"He went to the local junior college," the mayor adds, "fell in with the wrong crowd...bunch of burnouts."

"I thought we'd been making progress," Rebecca continues, "and then abruptly we weren't."

"He disappeared for a couple of weeks," the mayor says. "Violated his parole...even I couldn't keep him out of jail that time."

"But he was eligible for a new pilot program at the Big Farm for addicts under twenty-one," Rebecca adds. "And against his case worker's advice—"

"It was that or prison," the mayor barks.

No one actually replies, "...and now he's dead," but the response hangs in the air just the same.

"Again, I'm truly sorry to hear about your son," I say, "but I imagine farming accidents aren't uncommon, and I still don't understand why I'm here."

"The results of the autopsy came back yesterday along with the toxicology report." The mayor moves from his well-upholstered chair to sit on the corner of his desk near me. "I had the autopsy done because I just couldn't understand how Sloan—naming him that was my wife's idea—could've been run over by a slow-moving tractor. The operator said he didn't see him, so I figured he must've been unconscious out in that cornfield, and I wanted to know why."

"And what was in the report?" I ask.

"The medical examiner found traces of opioids in his system, which is what he overdosed on the night he smashed his truck into a tree and got arrested for the second time."

"Once more, I'm really sorry," I say, "but that couldn't have come as much of a surprise, and I still don't see what any of this has to do with me."

"It was very much a surprise," the mayor vehemently replies. "Sloan had come home for Sunday dinner every week going on three months now. His eyes were always clear, and he sounded like his old self. The farm work was agreeing with him—said he was in the best shape of his life and even talked about playing ball again."

"So what then?" I ask. "Did he have a relapse?"

"It's possible," Rebecca says, "but the Farm is known for having very strict drug-screening protocols. One positive urine test, and he would've been sent back to prison. This is the only reported incident of a resident testing positive...though—"

"That's just speculation," interrupts the mayor.

"Though what?" I ask.

"Though there have been a few reports of disappearances."

"Disappearances?" Slim chimes in. "More like escapees. If I was forced to trade a drug-fueled lifestyle for eighty hours of farm work a week, I might not be so keen on sticking around either."

"I'm loath to agree with Officer Stretch back there," I say, "but that makes sense to me too. I'm surprised that more than just a few of the so-called residents haven't run off."

"But that's where the red flags start popping up for me," Rebecca replies. "One of the biggest problems for operations like these is keeping the drugs out. If their security is as good at keeping the contraband from getting in, then how are the residents escaping?"

"Couldn't they just vanish when they leave on Sunday nights?" I ask.

"They could," Rebecca says, "but from what I've heard, they have a buddy system. If they choose to leave the Farm on Sundays, then they're required to do so with at least one other resident, and if they don't both return, then it counts against the one who does."

"That's true," says the mayor. "Sloan always came to dinner with a friend—usually a skinny guy named Gus who was a couple of years older than him."

"So then couldn't they both just not report back together?" I ask.

"Again, they could," Rebecca answers, "but as I understand it—based on what little I've been told— that's never happened. These disappearances have been just one individual at a time, usually last seen on a weekday at the Farm. And this is the biggest red flag of all: so far none of the patients who've disappeared have resurfaced."

"That does seem odd," I say.

"You bet it is," Rebecca replies. "Typically addicts who disappear from a treatment program turn up a week or so later—either in the hospital or under arrest. It's extremely rare that a patient who disappears remains disappeared."

"Now, Becky," the mayor says in a calming voice, "don't go fomenting fear of a program that has had so much success. Despite what happened to my son, the Big Farm has done a lot to help this community."

"Then why aren't they more transparent about how exactly they're helping?" Rebecca asks. "All I know about the goings-on out at the Farm is that most of the residents seem to get better but not quite well enough to leave…at least not in a timely manner unless they happen to disappear."

"The residents get free room and board," the mayor responds. "Why wouldn't they want to stay?"

"The residents of a prison get free room and board too," Rebecca replies, "and they can't wait to go."

"Okay," I speak up, "I feel like we're swimming out of my depth now. You have my condolences, but this has nothing to do with me, and there's no way I can help here."

"Actually," the mayor begins, "because this has nothing to do with you is part of the reason that you can help."

"I don't know what you're going to tell me next," I say, "but I'm pretty sure I'm not going to like it."

"Listen, this is a small town."

"So I've been told."

"The Big Farm isn't in the township limits," the mayor continues, "so I can't dispatch my municipal police officers to investigate this matter—even if I wanted to…which I don't. Like I said, the Farm has done great things for the community, so I don't want to cause undue difficulties for them, but as a father, I want some answers."

"Isn't there a county sheriff that you could lean on to look into this…or the state police? Somebody must be a better choice than me. As you said, my only qualification appears to be that I'm unaffiliated."

"The sheriff is as reluctant to stir up trouble as I am, and as for the state troopers…they're better at issuing speeding tickets on the Interstate than investigating. But being unaffiliated isn't your only qualification. You're also thought of as something of a celebrity—which can open a lot of doors and a lot of mouths in these parts."

"While I appreciate your kind words, I still think I'm woefully underqualified—I'm just a romance writer after all."

"Funny," the mayor says, "I think of you more as a writer of adventure stories with a hint of mystery. Anyway, I'm not asking you to conduct an actual investigation, and I'm certainly not asking you to do anything in an official capacity—just go ask a few questions and see what you can find out. Perhaps you could start this afternoon."

"I can't, I have plans this afternoon."

"Right, at that exclusive, tucked-away shooting club that also happens to be outside the township's limits. Aren't you meeting Dr. Weize, the Big Farm's psychiatrist, for some target shooting?"

"Skeet shooting. Word really does travel fast in a small town."

"It's about the only thing that does," Slim says.

"Sloan was a nice kid," Rebecca adds.

"Then I suppose I ought to at least try to help...lest my soul become imperiled and all that."

Chapter 8

Once again I ford the massive mud puddle and drive up to the gatehouse. It's a different guard today, but before I come to a complete stop, he presses the button to open the gate. "I know who you are, Mr. Payley. Go on up to the main house. They're expecting you."

When I pull up, I see Geoff and Dr. Weize waiting for me on the front steps, shotguns resting against their shoulders. As the valet takes my car, the two make their way over, acting as if they were intending to walk in my direction regardless of whether I happened to be standing there or not.

"Sorry, I'm late. I had an unexpected meeting."

"No problem," Geoff replies. "We just finished up a luncheon ourselves."

"I see that you both have double-barrel, break-action shotguns," I say.

"You sound rather knowledgeable about firearms for someone who claims to have never shot one," Dr. Weize replies.

"I've never fired a gun before, but I've written about them a time or two."

"Dr. Weize has a side-by-side model," Geoff explains, "whereas I prefer an over-and-under."

"Are there any pump-action shotguns available?" I ask.

"No," Dr. Weize says definitively.

"Those are sort of frowned upon at this club," Geoff says. "Come on, we'll get you all squared away at the range."

We walk over to a nearby golf cart where a driver waits behind the wheel. Dr. Weize takes the passenger's seat; Geoff and I sit in the two rear-facing seats on the back. The cart's electric motor whirs to life, and we're whisked away down a paved path that winds past a stand of trees and a small pond.

"Did you do any deer or bird hunting this morning?" I ask.

"No," Geoff answers, "deer and waterfowl aren't in season until later in the year."

"Then what do you hunt this time of year?"

"Me personally…not much of anything. I just like walking around with a gun and occasionally shooting at a target. I believe groundhogs are free game, and I think squirrel season starts soon, but who the hell wants to shoot at a bunch of rodents?"

"There's a coyote hunt every Friday night," Dr. Weize says over his shoulder, "but they hardly ever bag one."

The cart comes to a stop near a semicircle track. A shed is located at each end of the half circle, the nearer slightly taller than the farther and about forty yards apart from one another. A man in a white uniform and an orange safety vest approaches. As he nears, I notice that he has an eyepatch.

Geoff stands up from the cart. "Here comes the rangemaster now."

Dr. Weize catches me eyeing the eyepatch. "I'm told that he lost the eye during a duel somewhere in the

Caribbean. As I understand it, he wears the patch, rather than a glass eye, as sort of a badge of honor."

"Why would he want to honor a duel that he lost?" I ask in a whisper.

"No, no," the doctor clarifies, "he lost his eye, but his opponent lost the duel—along with his life…or so the story goes."

"Good afternoon, gentlemen," says the rangemaster, which by the way, as job titles go, is a pretty good one. "It's an excellent day for skeet shooting. First let me give you a little background about this sport. It was developed in the 1920s by William Foster who is known as the Father of Skeet. He originally conceived the course as a full circle with a trap firing skeet at the twelve o'clock position; however, a chicken farm next door prevented him from shooting in half the clock face's direction, so the circle was made into a semicircle with two traps. Think of it…a sport invented to simulate hunting wild birds stymied by domesticated birds."

"A fowl irony to be sure," I say. "Can you tell me where the word 'skeet' comes from?"

"I believe it's derived from the Norwegian word for 'shoot,' " Dr. Weize answers, "which is 'skyte' if I'm not mistaken, so when you use the phrase skeet shooting, you're really saying shoot shooting…in a manner of speaking."

"Yes, that's correct," confirms the rangemaster.

"Very impressive," I say. "You really are something of a philologist."

"The term was coined by Gertrude Hurlbutt in 1926 as part of a contest sponsored by the *National Sportsman* magazine," the rangemaster continues.

"During the Second World War, the US military used skeet to train its gunners on how to lead flying targets. Okay, that's enough of the history lesson. Let's go crack some clay pigeons."

Upon informing the rangemaster that I've never fired a gun before, which he found both amusing and sad, he outfits me with an over-and-under that looks very similar to Geoff's shotgun. He assures me that it's a good firearm for a middle-aged beginner. Given my novice status, we opt to forgo the formal scoring rules of skeet shooting and instead take turns firing from different positions along the track.

Each time, Geoff and Dr. Weize shoot at two clay pigeons. One launched about ten feet high from a trap in the high house, and the other launched about three feet off the ground from the low house. Geoff hits most of his low targets and misses most of the high ones. Dr. Weize does better with the high targets, but hits enough of each to demonstrate that he is clearly the more accomplished shooter. As for me, I miss everything my first few turns, even though I'm given two shots to fire at just one clay pigeon. I know enough to brace myself for the kick of the shotgun in my shoulder, but what surprises me is just how loud the report of the gun is when you're the one firing it; the thunderclap completely unnerves me the first couple of times. However, with some pointers from the rangemaster— "squeeze the trigger, don't tug at it" and "aim for where the target will be, not where it is"—I manage to hit a few clay pigeons in a row and graduate to trying to hit two at a time like Geoff and Dr. Weize.

After our first round, Geoff proposes a wager. "Let's make this a little more interesting. Dr. Weize is the best shot of the three of us, and Weston, no offense, you're the worst, though doing remarkably well for your first time. There are seven stations along the track. Let's have Weston shoot from all seven, I'll shoot from six, and Dr. Weize, you can shoot from five. Whoever breaks the most pigeons wins."

"That sounds agreeable," says Dr. Weize, "but what are the stakes?"

"I don't know," Geoff says. "How about ten thousand dollars paid to the winner to be split by the two losers?"

"I don't want to speak for Dr. Weize," I say, "but that's a bit too rich for my blood. Besides, why not try gambling for something more motivating than money?"

"What do you have in mind?" asks Geoff.

"Well," I begin, not quite sure where I'm going with this, "we're each successful in our respective fields—Geoff, you as a businessman, Dr. Weize, you as a professor, and me as a novelist. I suspect each of us has learned some interesting things along the way that have helped us succeed—the type of things that aren't typically taught and that someone on the outside of our chosen fields looking in would be surprised to know. I suggest that the two losers divulge one such secret to the winner—something provocative."

"Oh, that does sound rather intriguing," Dr. Weize says.

"But how would we know if what the losers tell the winner is sufficiently, as you said, provocative?" Geoff asks.

"It would have to be a gentlemen's agreement, of course," I answer. "However, since none of us share the same field, there's no real threat that the winner could use the information against the losers."

"Besides," Dr. Weize adds, "I know from years of listening to patients' darkest secrets that confession is good for the psyche."

"Okay," Geoff says hesitantly, "I'm more accustomed to wagers in which I only stand to lose a few grand, but I suppose I ought to get out of my comfort zone every now and then, so I'm in. Weston, you'll be shooting both first and last."

I shoot from the first station and miss both targets. Geoff shoots next, starting at the same station, and hits the low target but misses the high one. Dr. Weize opts to start from station two, and he hits both targets.

We shoot from the next several stations around the track. Dr. Weize only misses one clay pigeon for a total of nine hits. Geoff, true to form, makes all his low targets but only half of his high ones, also for a total of nine hits. After my first pair of misses, I make at least one hit at the next five stations, and thrice I manage to hit both pigeons, for a total of eight hits going into the final station where I'll be shooting alone.

As I take my position, I sense the tension in Dr. Weize and Geoff who are standing nearby. The rangemaster stands a little farther off. I hear his instructions in my head as I firmly grip the gun's stock but lightly rest my index finger against the trigger. The first clay pigeon is launched from the high house, and I hit it dead center, blasting it to pieces. I turn to see the second pigeon take a peculiar arc. I lead the target and fire. The pigeon appears to wobble slightly but then lands and rolls on its side for a ways.

"It looks like you end up with nine as well," Geoff says as he slaps me on the back. If I had one more round left in my shotgun, I'd be tempted to use it now and put a permanent end to all his backslapping.

"A three-way tie," Dr. Weize adds. "Most unexpected."

"Wait a moment, gentlemen." The rangemaster approaches. "That last pigeon landed oddly. I'd like to have a look at it."

The rangemaster jogs out into the field, locates the clay pigeon in question, inspects it, and then quickly returns.

"Just as I thought." The rangemaster shows us the clay pigeon, which is not completely intact. "They almost never roll like that unless they've been winged. You can see from the hole that some of the shot penetrated the pigeon. Even though the target didn't completely break apart, it still counts as a hit."

"I suppose that means you won," Geoff says sourly.

"Well done," says Dr. Weize. "You have the makings of a real marksman."

"Gentlemen, I'd like to congratulate all of you on an excellent round of shooting," the rangemaster says. "Now if you'll excuse me, I'll go police the field."

We watch in silence for a moment as the rangemaster jogs back out into the field and begins to pick up clay pigeon detritus.

Geoff is the first to speak. "I know a lot of rich people. Some of them are good people—philanthropists...people blessed with gifts in a particular area but otherwise normal and proud of it. But I also know other rich people who are arrogant beyond compare and whose only gift is that they were born into wealth. As you might imagine, these two factions of the upper crust don't get along so well, but no matter how much antipathy exists between them, none of them break the one cardinal rule of the rich community. As much as they might snipe about one another within our elite circle, they don't disparage its members to outsiders, because they know what the punishment is: ostracism…no more charitable donations…no more connections. People think you have to start with money to get rich, which is sort of true, but the real truth is that you have to know rich people. Business is all about connections—that's the secret."

With that Geoff turns and walks away, the barrel of his shotgun hanging down like a long tail. As he passes the golf cart, he calls out over his shoulder, "I feel like a walk. I'll meet you boys back at the main house."

"Success in business is less about what you know and more about who you know," Dr. Weize says derisively. "I'd hardly call that provocative."

"I've known Geoff a long time. Trust me—that admission came at a cost that was dear."

"Well, it was an interesting wager that you proposed. It shows you have a curious streak, which is a mark of intelligence."

"Thank you, but why does it feel a bit like you're stalling?"

"See," says Dr. Weize with a wry smile, "I knew you were intelligent. Yes, I am stalling somewhat because I can't think of any profound secret to divulge. Frankly, Geoff shot as well as I thought he would, but I figured I wouldn't miss any of my targets, and I hadn't anticipated that your shooting would improve so quickly."

"Thanks again, and it's not a problem if you can't—"

"No, no," Dr. Weize interrupts as I'd hoped he would. "A bet is a bet, and I'm a man of my word, but I'm afraid I have to leave now for an appointment. How about this: you're clearly an inquisitive person, as all good writers should be, and judging from your line of questioning last night, you have a particular curiosity about my work, so why don't you come out to the Big Farm tomorrow afternoon? I'll show you around a little, and we can chat some more. I can't have you sit in on any of my sessions, of course, but I can introduce you to a couple of my patients who would be amenable to answering any questions you might have."

"I'd like that."

"Splendid, that'll give me a chance to sleep on it and think of something provocative to share with you tomorrow. Who knows, maybe I'll wind up as a character in one of your books someday."

Chapter 9

"What's taking your brother so long?" Rebecca asks her youngest son as she sprinkles paprika on a tray of deviled eggs.

"I don't know," Lance answers without looking up from the handheld video game he's engrossed in.

"Can you please go find out?" she asks. "We're running late for the barbecue."

"Sure," the boy replies, leaving his spot next to the refrigerator and exiting into the living room.

"So then what happened after you won the skeet-shooting contest?" she asks me. "Which by the way, I'm still having a hard time picturing you shooting a shotgun."

"I have to admit," I say as I cut carrots on the countertop, "it was rather fun. Haven't you ever shot a shotgun before?"

"Sure, I used to go pheasant hunting with my dad, but then I'm a simple small-town girl—not some big-city sophisticate."

"Need I remind you that I too am now a country mouse?"

"What you need to do is to finish your story before we go."

"I can't," I reply. "Dr. Weize had an appointment to get to, so he invited me to the Big Farm tomorrow to finish our conversation. I'm afraid my story is to be continued."

"That's great." Rebecca hands me a paprika-covered egg slice. "I've been angling for an invitation to the Big Farm for months now, and you manage to secure one in just an afternoon—well done."

"I was hoping for a somewhat more sinful show of appreciation than a deviled egg." I begin noshing the egg slice.

"Keep playing your cards right, and you'll be more appreciated than you can handle this weekend while the boys are with my sister," she tells me with a devilish grin.

"I do respond better to carrots than sticks." I return to my cutting.

Rebecca snatches a carrot from the counter and whispers, "Then I'll show you someplace new to put your carrot stick." She holds the carrot perpendicular to her lips, suggestively signaling me to keep quiet.

"In that case, I suppose I should ask what I can help with next."

"Can you please check to see if Lance checked on Vancy?"

"Sure thing." I exit the kitchen. In the living room, I find that Lance has traded leaning against the refrigerator for leaning against the bottom of the staircase.

"Is your brother almost ready?"

"I went up to his room," Lance informs me without looking up from his game, "but he told me to 'go away.' "

"Okay." I begin to climb the stairs. "I'll check on him."

I knock on Van's ajar door and stick my head inside. I wish I hadn't. He's sprawled out on his bed, scrutinizing a glossy magazine and wearing a single tube sock...not on either of his feet. He sees me see him before I can pull my head back out.

"I'm going to need a judgment-free moment right now," Van tells me with a diffident voice.

"You got it," I say from the other side of his door. "Sorry to interrupt...I mean intrude...I mean just meet us downstairs when you're done...I mean ready...you know what I mean."

I descend the stairs and reach through the banister to tousle Lance's hair. "Your brother will be down soon."

Back in the kitchen, Rebecca is packing up the food. "Is Vancy dressed yet?"

"Partially," I answer. "He just needs another minute."

Chapter 10

I park in Rebecca's driveway. Lance is asleep in the backseat, but that doesn't prevent Van from opening his door before I've come to a complete stop and then slamming it shut as he gets out.

"Where's my game?" Lance asks groggily as he wakes up.

"I've got it up here, sweetie," Rebecca answers from the passenger's seat.

"Can I have it?"

"Not until we get inside...check that." Rebecca takes note of the clock on the dashboard. "It's late, and you've got school tomorrow, so no more video games tonight."

"Aw...Mom."

"Don't 'aw Mom' me." You've spent plenty of time playing that game today...Operation Brain Rot is officially over for the evening."

"Okay."

"Now tell Weston goodnight and then go inside. Vancy's already unlocked the front door for you."

"Goodnight, East-Off." Lance pats my shoulder and then exits the car.

"East-Off?" Rebecca asks. "That's a new one."

"He's been having wordplay fun with opposites lately."

"That's cute."

"Cuter than if my name was Ascend-Vomit."

"You're a good influence on him."

"You know, because then the opposite would be Dip-Shit…not that Ascend-Vomit is any prize of a name."

"No, I get it. That whole you're-a-good-influence thing is really just a working hypothesis."

"I like your boys." I suppress the urge to blurt out other opposite names that pop into my head. "And one of your boys likes me, so that's not a terrible ratio."

"Vancy will come around."

"Sure, like when he's forty…or I'm dead, whichever comes first."

"You always have such an optimistic outlook," she says, wrinkling her nose. "Anyway, thanks for coming with us tonight to the barbecue."

"Not a problem. I like barbecue."

"No, I mean meeting all my friends. I've told them a lot about you, so they've really been wanting meet you."

"They seem like nice people."

"You're nice people too." She squeezes my hand. "Do you want to come in for a bit?"

"I do, but you've got to get your boys to bed, and I'd just be in the way. I'll stop by tomorrow night after you drop them off at your sister's…though I might be a little late if it's a cloudless night."

"I can hardly wait to hear what that has to do with anything." She gives me a goodnight kiss.

Chapter 11

The Big Farm looks to me a lot like a plantation. Cornfields stretch past the horizon in almost every direction. People move to and fro, entering one outbuilding and exiting another, like ants in a formicarium. It all seems rather informal; I was expecting something more akin to the chain gangs in *Cool Hand Luke*.

A young man walks by as I get out of my car. "Excuse me, do you know where I could find Dr. Weize's office?"

"Dr. Weize." The young man sounds confused. "Are you talking about Dr. Jude?"

"Possibly…I don't know his first name. He's a psychiatrist here."

"Sure—that's Jude the headshrinker. He holds his group sessions in the Shed."

I point to a nearby barn that an enormous tractor is slowly pulling into. "Is that the shed?"

"No, that's just a barn…or a machine shed, so I guess you're not too far off, but that farmhouse on the hill over yonder is the 'Shed'…or at least that's what we call it."

"If Dr. Weize…I mean, Jude's office is in the house, then where do you all stay?"

"You mean us recoverers? Wherever we want. They built some barracks a while back that we can bunk in, but I prefer to sleep under the stars, so a group of us camp down by the creek whenever the weather permits."

"That does sound rather pleasant."

"Beats sleeping in a crack house," the young man replies with a wave. "I've got chores to do, but go on over to the Shed, and they'll get you fixed up."

"Thank you kindly." I return his wave and walk toward the farmhouse. I espy Dr. Weize sitting in a rocking chair on the veranda. He spots me as I approach and rises to greet me.

"Good afternoon, Mr. Payley."

"A good afternoon to you, Dr. Weize…or should I call you Dr. Jude?"

"Sure, Weston, we're all on a first-name basis here," he says as we shake hands. "For the team leaders, as we euphemistically refer to them, who are mostly erstwhile prison guards, it's a holdover of not wanting to be looked up by ex-cons on the outside; however, for me, I find that the formality of surnames can be a barrier to my work. Most of my patients feel more comfortable using first names or even sobriquets."

"Yes, a young man I spoke to a moment ago referred to you as the headshrinker."

"Frankly, I find all this nicknaming a bit too cornpone for comfort, but I must admit that I've always rather enjoyed that particular moniker." Jude leads me into the house. "I just finished a session, so I have some time if you'd like to chat in my office."

The farmhouse's interior is a mashup of old-fashioned and contemporary. In the kitchen, an energy-efficient, stainless-steel refrigerator stands next to a butcher-block counter inset with a porcelain basin sink.

In the living room, which serves as a waiting room, atop an antique coffee table that Abraham Lincoln might've once rested his feet upon sits a whisper-quiet, bladeless fan with copies of *Psychology Today* strewn around it.

We enter Jude's office, which looks as if it might've been the dining room, and he pulls the pocket doors closed behind us. He sits in a swivel chair behind his desk, whose sole purpose appears to be showcasing all manner of knickknacks and bric-a-brac. I take a seat on the couch rather than in one of the folding chairs that clutter the room.

"Should I lie down?" I ask facetiously.

"If you feel like unburdening yourself," Jude replies, seeming to regard my question as serious. "Just be sure to keep your head at the proper end of the couch as the other end has seen many a muddy boot."

"So what's with all the gewgaws on your desk?"

"These are gifts from former patients who, with my help, overcame their various addictions." Jude picks up a snow globe with a butterfly inside, which doesn't make any sense at all. "Their purpose is twofold. We use them as talking tokens in group sessions—patients pass them to whoever's turn it is to speak."

"What's the second fold?"

"Trophies." Jude replaces the snow globe on his desk in the exact spot where he'd taken it from, making sure it has the same orientation as before. "When my patients realize that each of these trinkets represents a former patient who has undergone a successful treatment program, this collection of baubles becomes more impressive than all the diplomas hanging on the wall behind me."

I take note of said diplomas over his shoulder. He went to grad school at the same university where he's now a professor.

"Patient treatment is what I'd most like to talk with you about."

"Before we get into that, let me share with you the provocative thought I had last night about my field." Jude picks up a matryoshka nesting doll. "After all, I am the one holding a talking token."

"Then by all means…share away."

"I'm afraid that on the face of it, what I have to share won't sound any more provocative than Geoff's admission that prospering in business is about who you know, so I ask for your forbearance. Religion is no longer the opiate of the masses…opioids are. Drug counseling is one of the few careers in which an absolute success would mean the end of the profession, but unfortunately none of my colleagues are concerned about job security. That's the dirty little secret that all of us know. We're fighting a war that we'll never win."

"But it seems as if you're winning a lot of battles here…more than most."

"Perhaps it's my success that emboldens my candor. I've found a way to help those who want help, but if I'm being honest, this farm…these bucolic environs probably do more to mend the minds of my patients than my therapy does."

"How so?"

"I use unpleasant elements of my patients' childhoods to make negative associations with their drug habits, and it works to a degree, but this place reminds them of the positive aspects of their childhoods, and positive reinforcement is much more effective than negative."

"This community has strong agrarian roots, but all your patients couldn't have grown up on farms."

"No, of course not. In fact, for some of our patients, this is the first time they've ever been on a working farm; however, most of our patients grew up in the towns around here or places like them, and in their childhoods, the idealized notion of the farm as a self-sufficient, utopian haven became engrained. It's simply part of their autochthonous zeitgeist."

"Autochthonous zeitgeist?" The bait is in the water, and I've gotten a few nibbles, but I haven't landed the fish yet. "You just went from A to Z, but I don't think I understood what was in between."

"Forgive me." The good doctor returns the nesting doll back to his desk. "I was trying to sound impressive because I feel rather foolish admitting this out loud, which, as I understood from the nature of our wager yesterday, satisfies the requirements of the stakes."

"Indeed it does, but I want to make sure I understand you. Are you telling me that your success here couldn't be replicated in a less pastoral setting?"

"I can't tell you that with any certainty, but I have my suspicions that it could not, which I'll be sure to omit when the time comes to publish. Others will use my techniques, and obviously I wish them success, but if they don't achieve the same sort of success that I've had here, then I imagine that will reflect poorly on the administrators of my methods rather than the methods themselves, since I've unequivocally demonstrated the possibility of their success."

"And in the process, further enhance your reputation," I add.

"Perhaps, but as I've already fulfilled my obligation from our wager, you'll understand if I'm disinclined to make any further admissions today."

"Just one last question...can you tell me what happened to a patient of yours—Sloan McCormick?"

"Unfortunate business that. He was an affable young man who was making great progress, and then suddenly...well, I suppose if you're asking the question, you know the rest."

"I don't know very much at all...only that he died in a farming accident out here and that opioids were found in his system."

"As I said, most unfortunate...but as I'm sure you can appreciate, these things do sometimes happen. The vicissitudes of an addict can surprise even the most seasoned therapist. Regrettably, I'm not at liberty to share any more than that as it's still an ongoing investigation."

"My understanding is that there hasn't been much of an investigation."

"As you might imagine, the authorities seldom update me on their inquiries." Jude stands. "Now, you must excuse me as I have another session that begins soon, and I need to review my notes beforehand."

"No problem." I rise to leave. "I appreciate your time."

"It was good to see you again." Jude walks around his desk and slides open the pocket doors. "I hope to see you soon at the club, though I don't expect that I'll be making any more wagers."

"I got lucky is all."

"I've heard it said that it's better to be lucky than good." Jude shakes my hand. "I promised yesterday that I would introduce you to a couple of my patients who I didn't think would be averse to talking with you; however, I'm afraid I'm a bit pressed for time, so I won't be able to offer you a formal introduction, but I asked two of my patients from my earlier group session to stay and work on the grounds around the house this afternoon in case you had any questions for them, though I'll thank you to confine your questions about their treatment to generalities and refrain from asking them anything specific about what we discuss in session."

"Sure, I understand—thanks again." I make my way toward the front door.

The air outside is muggy compared to the cool air inside. I hear a lawnmower from around the side of the house, so I walk the length of the porch and take a look. Figures—it's Rebecca's ex-husband. What are the odds? Our meeting last time went well enough, but I don't want to tempt fate by asking Rodney a bunch of questions about his treatment. Besides, the smell of the freshly cut grass and the fumes from the gas-powered mower are causing my sinuses to clog…ah, fresh air. I walk to the other side of the porch and see a young man who thankfully I don't recognize. He's lackadaisically trimming a bush in front of a large propane tank.

I descend the porch steps and saunter in his general direction, trying to look casual. It's trickier than I would've thought to appear as if I'm walking without purpose; I suppose I need to work on my moseying skills. I admire the stature of the corn that surrounds the yard, which very well could be as high as an elephant's eye. The young man spots me as I approach and lowers his hedge shears.

"Can I help you, mister?"

"What kind of bush is that?" I ask, trying to strike up a conversation.

"I'm not sure…I just trim 'em, you know."

"I read you." I try a different tack. "So what do they use all that propane for?"

"You must be that guy that Dr. Jude said might have some questions for me. I gotta tell ya—these ain't the sort of questions I figured you'd be asking. The propane is mostly for heat in the winter, but it can also be used to power the generators when the electricity goes out."

"Does that happen often?"

"Now and then…it's to be expected on a farm so far from the town limits, but it's nice to know we got a backup plan in place."

"You guys are fairly self-sufficient out here."

"I reckon we are…with the generators for electricity and the well for drinking water, we're not really dependent on the town's utilities."

"This place seems like an advantageous arrangement all around—your room and board are covered, and you're paid a decent wage."

The young man eyes my leather loafers. "I don't know about 'decent.' "

"Since you have all your expenses covered, I figure even minimum wage would be fairly good."

"I figure it would be too, but that ain't what they're payin' us." The young man spits on the ground. "We get a lot less."

"Is that legal?"

"They got different laws for farm workers, but then like you said, out here we ain't got nothin' to spend our money on anyhow."

"Maybe you all should unionize." I chuckle, but he doesn't seem amused. "Otherwise though, you feel like you're being treated well out here…nothing out of the ordinary going on?"

"Like what?"

"I don't know." I really don't; I'm just fishing again. "Like maybe what happened to Sloan McCormick."

"Sloan was a friend of mine, but one of the things they teach us out here is accountability. Sloan had a good thing going, but he made a bad choice, and he paid the price. I wish it was different—but it ain't."

"Did you know he was using?"

"No, but us addicts can get real good at hiding those types of things," he tells me with a bitter look.

"Just one more question—do you know where I can find another friend of Sloan's named Gus?"

"He's probably over in the machine shed." The young man goes back to using his hedge shears, now with more intensity than before. "You probably saw it on your way in, so you can stop by on your way out."

"Thanks."

I stop in the machine shed on my way back to my car, but I don't see anyone. It's just me and a massive green tractor that looks like it could tow a fleet of tanks. I climb up to have a look through the cab window. All manner of high-tech gear surrounds the driver's seat. I consider opening the door to the cab, but someone below calls up to me.

"She's a beauty, ain't she?"

I look down to see a thin man wearing a t-shirt covered in grease, wiping his hands with a rag that's even greasier than his shirt.

"I've never seen one of these up close before." I climb down. "They look a lot smaller from the Interstate. With all the gadgets in there, it seems like you'd almost have to be an astronaut to operate one."

"Nah, with the GPS system this one's got, it practically drives itself."

"Fascinating," I say and mean it. "My name is Weston, by the way."

"Gus, nice to meet you."

"You too—in fact, you're just who I was looking for when I came in here."

"Is that right? You ain't the law is you?"

"No, nothing like that. I'm a friend of Sloan's family."

"Funny, I don't recall ever seeing you at any of their Sunday dinners?"

"Well, more of a friend of a friend of the family. Working out here, I bet you two usually brought the corn on the cob to those dinners."

"That's field corn out there."

"Where else would corn be grown but in a field?" I ask with what I'm sure is a stupid expression on my face.

"No, you see ninety-nine percent of the corn grown in America isn't the type of corn that you eat on the cob. Most of it's used for animal feed, which is why it's sometimes called cow corn, but it can also be processed to make other things, like corn syrup and ethanol. Corn starch is even used to make chemical products, like plastics and adhesives. I hear it's even used to make fish bait."

"Cows eat it, cars run on it, fish get caught with it, and people get drunk on it. It would seem they don't call it king corn for nothing—maize truly is amazing. I guess the only thing corn isn't good for is keeping secrets…you know, because of all the ears."

"Yeah, I've heard all those corny jokes before. Listen, I got a lot of work to do, so—"

"What kind of work do you do out here?" Not a great question.

"As you can probably tell by my shirt, I'm a grease monkey."

"Sounds like good work—keeps you out of the sun I imagine."

"The machinery don't usually break down when it's just sittin' in here, but still…it beats detasseling."

"I hear that."

"Oh, you've detasseled corn before?" Gus asks skeptically.

"Not per se, but I've had my share of tough jobs."

"Tough jobs, huh…so if you ain't the law, then what do you do for a living?"

"I'm a writer."

"Is that right?" Gus asks with a bemused expression. "What sorts of things do you write?"

"Novels…adventure stories mostly." I'm starting to feel like I'm on the wrong end of an interrogation. "The odd romance now and then."

"I wouldn't exactly call that a tough job, but then, for me at least, I wouldn't call it easy either."

"Everything is a matter of perspective. You writing novels would probably be easier for you than me working on tractors."

"Maybe…so what do you want to know about Slow?"

"Slow?"

"That's what we called him…those of us who knew him well."

"Why, was he a slow worker?"

"No, he was a good worker…a good guy. He just had this real deliberate way about him, like when he spoke. You'd ask him a question, and it would take him a moment to collect his thoughts, but then his answer would be, you know, thoughtful."

"Doesn't sound like the kind of guy to suddenly rush back into drug use."

"No, it doesn't. We all got our problems…each has our own demons chasing after us, but Sloan seemed like he was committed to the straight and narrow path. He was the best of us."

"A guy I just talked to said that addicts are good at hiding those sorts of things…even from the people closest to them."

"Yeah, that's true enough." Gus sticks his hand into his pocket. "But Slow was always the first to volunteer for more work…the first to show up for our group sessions. When I'd heard he'd been run over by a tractor, I figured he'd collapsed from heatstroke in the cornfield and hit his head on a rock or something—it can get mighty humid out in those fields—but then when they said he had opioids in his system…I just couldn't believe it."

Gus pulls a handful of capsules from his pocket and holds them up for me to see. I have no idea what I'm looking at.

"Are those opioids?"

"No, they're vitamins. They give us one each morning with breakfast. They say that the drugs we took robbed our bodies of nutrients, and that these will help to restore our health, but I never take them. I've spent too much of my life popping pills already. So I'd save them up and give them to Slow. That's how committed he was. He wanted to get better as soon as he could."

I take one of the capsules from Gus and examine it closely. It doesn't look anything like the multivitamins I take, but then mine are for men over fifty.

"Did Dr. Jude prescribe these?"

"They're just vitamins...no prescription necessary. They put them in little paper cups on our trays in the cafeteria."

"But does Dr. Jude know about these?"

"I guess so. It ain't like they're a big secret. Nobody watches us to make sure we take them or anything. They're recommended but not required, which is why I was able to save so many of them for Slow."

"Can I keep this one?"

"Suit yourself. I've just been pocketing these out of habit...hoping that maybe Slow will want them someday."

"He sounds like a nice kid. I'm sorry I didn't know him better."

Chapter 12

I drive the dusty backroads to see my oldest friend, Edwin Hubert. I'd feel remiss for not mentioning him earlier, except that he's somewhere on the spectrum between a recluse and a hermit, so I like to give him his privacy. I've only seen him twice since I moved here, despite him residing—at least sometimes—only twenty minutes away from my new house. We became pals one summer when we were both twelve, and I was visiting my granddad. He introduced himself as an umbraphile. I didn't know what that was, but I was pretty sure we were going to be good friends.

I met him just after some teenage boys had stolen a telescope he'd bought from the back of a comic book. They used the lens to start a fire that ended up melting the plastic telescope. Ed made me a confederate in his plan to exact revenge. He knew the boys usually hung out at the arcade, so he had me go in alone one day to play Space Invaders, which I was pretty good at because there was an arcade across the street from the school I went to in the city. Anyway, one of these older boys saw me playing, figured I wasn't any good on account of me being a younger kid that he hadn't seen before, and challenged me to a game with a five-dollar bet—high stakes in those days.

I accepted the bet and beat him, but of course, he wouldn't pay up, which Ed warned me would happen, so with his friends crowding around, he challenged me to a double-or-nothing match. Again Ed had warned me that this was the crew's modus operandi: if one of them ever lost a bet in the arcade, the others stood around the victor and intimidated him into a rematch until either he lost a double-or-nothing rematch and all was square or he walked away with his winnings and then they would strong-arm rob him when he left.

I declined the rematch, telling my opponent that he could keep the money he owed me, as I knew he was good for it and that we could have our double-or-nothing game on some future occasion. When one of the other boys asked why I was in such a hurry to leave, I told them that I was on my way to watch a solar eclipse, which of course there wasn't. I had to explain to them what a solar eclipse was, and then I mentioned that my father was an astronomer. (Edwin's dad was really the astronomer, though of an amateur standing.) I further explained that he had told me if you stared at a solar eclipse for long enough, you'd see whatever you most desired to see in all the world. The older boys just laughed, but I could tell that they partially believed me—imbeciles.

I returned the next day to the arcade, and the boys cornered me again. They asked how my solar eclipse watching went. I informed them that it had worked; I saw what I most wanted to see. Which was…the boys had asked. A naked Princess Leia, obviously. This time they completely believed me—the prospect of a nude space princess making all things plausible. I then told them that there was another solar eclipse that afternoon, which of course there was. I barely got the words out before the older boys raced out of the arcade.

I heard later that all the boys suffered temporary retinal damage and that the oldest boy developed a permanent visual impairment in one eye, though that same boy told people that he actually did see a nude Princess Leia dancing in the sun, so maybe it wasn't such a bad deal. Boys can be callous...what can you do?

Ed and I remained pen pals after my granddad passed, and then we reconnected when we went to the same college. He'd studied astronomy, among other things; he's pretty much the smartest person I know—but a complete social moron. We'd had wonderful, far-reaching discussions in our letters, but then when we got together on campus, we'd only talked about the things that happened all those summers ago...if that.

Anyway, during grad school he'd helped install a radio telescope with a massive radar dish out in the middle of nowhere. The university's official line, if anyone bothered to inquire, was that the remote location for the telescope had been chosen because it was far away from the light pollution of the campus and surrounding city, which was a lie, of course. Since it's a radio telescope, it works just as well during the day as it does at night. It wasn't set up to scan the cosmos for undiscovered stars but rather to scan for possible incoming missiles fired during the Cold War that could've threatened the nearby air force base, which undoubtedly had missiles of its own.

When the Cold War thawed, the base was closed, and the dish was all but abandoned, though Ed volunteered to stay on in order to continue his postdoc research...and because, after he finished his dissertation, he didn't have anywhere else to go, since he'd decided long before that he wasn't cut out for a university teaching position. The university agreed, in part, to keep up the charade of science but mostly because they just didn't care. I don't know if they even realize that anyone still uses the now antiquated telescope.

Ed's putative residence, which he mostly just stays at when the weather turns really cold, is whatever sublease he can find on campus from a recent dropout, but he spends most of his time living inside the base of the large telescope, and I know he'll be out tonight staring through his own optical telescope, as there's not a cloud in the sky.

I navigate down the dark dirt road. The trees on either side act as a windbreak, so the drive is eerily quiet. I park in front of the heavy chain that's suspended by two vertical railroad ties that flank the road. If not for the sign, which succinctly reads KEEP OUT, that dangles from the middle of the rusty chain, a driver could easily miss seeing it at night and hit the chain with the grill of his vehicle, likely collapsing the hood of his car to the engine block.

I kill the engine and get out. I step over the chain and make the short walk to the clearing where the telescope is located. A chain-link fence blocks the way, and another sign reads University Property—Trespassers Will Be Prosecuted!

I walk into the woods a bit, beyond the end of the fence, and then back into the clearing. Ed told me once that the university had originally intended to enclose the telescope within a complete perimeter fence, but because the surrounding woods were so thick and the telescope so well hidden from the main road, it was deemed unnecessary; they saved three-quarters of the cost of the fence by putting up only one side. I wonder what the savings on the fence was compared to the astronomical cost of the telescope.

As I'd anticipated, I find Ed sitting in a lawn chair, staring into the eyepiece of his stubby refractor telescope, which looks absurd next to the colossal radio telescope.

"A good night for stargazing," I say as I approach.

"Actually, Weston," Ed replies without looking up from the eyepiece, "it's a good night for seeing Mars."

"How did you know I was here?"

"I saw your headlights through the trees."

"But how did you know it was me?"

"You always walk like someone who's trying to sound quiet but can't quite manage it." Ed stands up. "Mars is in retrograde tonight. Care to have a look?"

"Sure." I sit down and look through the eyepiece. "I've always wanted to see a Martian."

"Let me know if you spot one."

"So far all I see is a vast bloody desert."

"Actually, our blood is red for the same reason the surface of Mars is red—the result of the chemical reaction between iron and oxygen. Beautiful, isn't it?"

"In its way, but I wouldn't want to vacation there."

"So what brings you out here tonight?"

"I wanted to ask you about a professor at the university, who I discovered today was also a grad student there about the same time as you...see if your paths ever crossed."

"Mine is the sin of indifference." It bugs me when Ed talks like that. "I'm sure I crossed paths with many people while I was on campus but failed to take notice.

Besides, the student body there is larger than the population of the town here."

"Sure, I figured it was a long shot, but I thought I'd ask anyway."

"Well, actually you haven't asked yet...what's this professor's name?"

"Dr. Jude Weize." I get out of the lawn chair. "It looks like the Red Planet has drifted out of view."

"Let me check." Ed reclaims the chair and looks into the eyepiece.

"I'm not an astronomer, but I know when I can't see a planet anymore."

"No, I meant I'm checking to see if I can recall that name." Ed adjusts the telescope slightly. He's got a terrific memory, but he sort of needs a running start to remember some things. "Is there anything that you can tell me about him?"

"He's a psychology professor currently on sabbatical."

"That doesn't help. If I knew him at all, it would've been years ago. Can you tell me what he was like then—any specific interests he might've had?"

"I just met him, so...wait, his avocation is philately."

"Stamp collecting...that's helpful. I tend to remember people who collect things."

"Then you did know him."

"No...sorry." Ed looks intently into the telescope's eyepiece. "I am certain that I did not. I wouldn't have forgotten a fellow obsessive." Ed has a comprehensive collection of Fantastic Four comic books and memorabilia—even recordings of the 1975 radio show that featured Bill Murray as the voice of the Human

Torch—just don't ask him about the movies. "Why are you so interested in this psychology professor?" Ed asks, without sounding particularly interested himself.

"Just a hunch...I'm looking into a somewhat suspicious death of a young man at the Big Farm—this drug rehab outfit that has sort of a cult vibe to it. I think Weize might be at the center of it."

"Of the cult?" Ed looks up and blinks.

"Well, it's not a cult—in fact, most people in town think they're doing a lot of good—that's just the vibe I get."

"Your hunch." Ed looks down again.

"Right, my gut instinct."

"Sometimes feelings that you think emanate from your gut may actually originate from other parts of your anatomy."

"What's that supposed to mean?"

"That I suspect, in an effort to play the hero, your thinking might be somewhat impaired on this matter."

"Oh really, and what makes you say that?"

"The barbecue last night—meeting your girlfriend's friends for the first time is a big step in a relationship...you two must be getting serious."

"And how do you know about any of that?"

"Social media." Ed twists a knob on his telescope. "But it's all just a hunch...I could very well be mistaken."

"I think you are. Although admittedly I have been spending a lot of time with my girlfriend—by the way, people over fifty don't use that term—and I do have plans to see her later this evening, so I get what you're saying."

"It can take but a small smudge on a tiny lens to occlude an entire galaxy."

"No, I understand…please, spare me the astronomy analogies."

"Anything else I can help you with then?"

"Maybe." I fish the vitamin supplement out of my pocket. "Do you still have any contacts on campus who could examine this capsule for me?"

"I can have a look at it."

"I need a chemist…I thought you were a physicist."

"Actually I'm a cosmologist, but everything is chemistry."

"You know, you use the word 'actually' an awful lot."

Chapter 13

I pull into Rebecca's driveway, and my headlights find her sitting in an Adirondack chair in the front yard. She waves at me as I park. I walk over to join her. "Nice night to be outside."

"Even nicer with a little vino." She holds up a glass of white wine. A set of binoculars rests on the arm of her chair.

"That bright one is Mars, which I believe is in retrograde."

"My, don't you know a lot about astronomy."

"I did a little research for my novel *Stargazing Spinster*," I fib as I sit down in the chair next to hers. The stars the title of that book refers to are celebrities.

Rebecca takes up the binoculars to get a better look at Mars. "There's an empty glass between our chairs next to the bottle of Chardonnay, and the plate covered with foil has some summer sausage and cheese if you're hungry."

I don't care for white wine, but I help myself to a slice of sausage and a couple cubes of what I think is Havarti. "Good cheese."

"Yeah, unless it comes on a pizza, my boys only eat Velveeta, so it's not often that I get to buy the cheese I like." She adjusts her binoculars. "It really is red."

"For the same reason our blood is red; it has to do with the interaction between iron and oxygen."

"Now you're just showing off." She lowers her binoculars and kisses me. Her lips taste salty and sweet.

We hold hands and lean back in our chairs to drink in the firmament. "You can't see stars like this in the city."

"No, you can't," she says.

We lounge in silence for several minutes—not talking, not moving…just being together. Then Rebecca suddenly sits straight up and holds her hand over her stomach.

"Are you okay?"

"Yes." She rubs her stomach. "Just a little indigestion I think; I guess my body isn't used to this sort of cheese anymore. Sorry, I didn't mean to ruin the moment."

"You didn't ruin anything, but I had to have an emergency appendectomy a few years ago, and it started with sudden stomach pain."

"It's passed now." She leans back once again. "Let's talk about something else. How did your visit to the Big Farm go today?"

"Fine, though I didn't really find what I was looking for."

"What were you looking for?"

"I don't know…clues to a mystery," I say sarcastically. "I suppose I was starting to feel like a character in one of my stories rather than a denizen of the real world."

"Perhaps it's good that you didn't find anything. Maybe that means Sloan's death happened just as the

McCormick family was told, which should give them some peace."

"Maybe so." I look up at the stars again. "Though I was hoping I could do more—and am disappointed that I couldn't, which is the reason I was reluctant to do anything in the first place...but I do have a friend looking into a small matter that may prove to be of some interest."

"Well, that sounds like something." Rebecca takes another sip of wine. "What's Dr. Weize like?"

"Typical professor type—full of himself and overly concerned with his reputation."

"Sage-on-the-stage syndrome...I'm familiar with it."

"All things considered though, he doesn't seem like a bad egghead to me. I get the sense that he genuinely wants to help his patients."

"That's good then." Rebecca sits up straight again.

"Stomachache back?"

"No, I think—" Rebecca stops midsentence, leans over the arm of her chair, and vomits onto the grass. "Wow...that was sexy."

"How much wine have you had?"

"I just opened the bottle."

"Then I'm taking you to the hospital."

"I don't think that's necessary."

"Trust me, if it's appendicitis, you'll want to get it taken care of sooner than later."

Chapter 14

I've been stranded in the waiting room, though it would be more accurate to call it the worrying room. The hospital staff wouldn't let me go back with Rebecca since I'm not family. I've just finished watching two episodes of *Gilligan's Island*—the first in color and the second in black and white, which seems backward. I have no idea what the plot of either was about...I think they're still marooned like me.

I check my watch; it's almost midnight. The only other person waiting with me is a drunk who came in with another drunk who looked as if he had a broken nose. He made a big fuss about not being allowed to accompany his friend into the emergency room. Rules are rules they told him. He cursed, went outside to smoke a cigarette, came back in, and then promptly fell asleep on the couch across from mine. I think maybe he's the one who broke his friend's nose.

I talk to the elderly nurse behind the glass, but after making a call, she tells me that there haven't been any updates, though she informs me with a smile that she's sure I'll hear something soon. Then I ask if she has the remote for the television hanging from the ceiling, and she gives me a nice big frown. She rummages around in her desk, finds the remote, and then carefully aims it at the TV through the little opening intended for payment of medical services rendered under the protective partition.

After several attempts, the screen changes to a continuous news network. Without asking if that'll do, the nurse tosses the remote back in its drawer and returns to her gossip magazine. I go back to my indentation on the couch and watch a segment about the flagging economy, then one about deteriorating US relations with the Middle East, then another about political corruption, and finally a story about the declining bee population.

I check my watch again; it's now into the small hours of the morning. I'd promised Rebecca that I wouldn't call her sister until she had some news about her condition, but I wonder if that promise has an expiration date. What if it gets late enough into the morning that it comes time to pick up her boys?

I return to the nurse's station to see about getting the TV changed back to *Gilligan's Island*, but just before I knock on the glass, Rebecca comes through the double doors separating the waiting room from the emergency room. She looks tired but otherwise fine. I hug her hard, and she hugs me back even harder.

"Are you okay?"

"Probably. It's not appendicitis, but the ER doctor—who's younger than me…when did they start making doctors younger than me?—isn't sure what's the matter, so he ordered a blood test, though he said his best guess is that it's likely run-of-the-mill abdominal distress brought on by eating spicy sausage and aging, which I think he thought would make me feel better."

"So what did the blood test show?"

"I won't get the results for three days." She looks at her watch. "Well, the day after tomorrow now."

"You were back there all that time just for a blood draw?"

"The blood draw only took a minute, waiting for the nurse who does the blood draws took an eternity."

"Doesn't the kid doctor know how to work a syringe?"

"I didn't feel like wandering up and down the hallways looking for him in the assless paper gown they made me wear." She pulls me in the direction of the exit. "I just want to leave…this wasn't the romantic evening I had in mind for us."

"I don't know…did they let you keep that assless gown?"

Chapter 15

I'm late for Rebecca's doctor's appointment. She, rather we, had to wait the remainder of the weekend for the lab to send her test results to her primary care physician. I was supposed to meet Rebecca at her doctor's office during her lunch hour, and though it's just a ten-minute drive from my place, I'm running twenty minutes late due to a seemingly never-ending train. Years ago, a friend of my granddad told me that Al Capone had once remarked to his father that he'd never rob a bank in this town because there was too high a risk of his getaway car being caught by a train. Clearly the story is apocryphal since Capone was never a bank robber, but the point still stands.

There's no rush hour in this town, but if you get stuck at a railroad crossing when one of these three-locomotive caravans goes by, it'll sure make you feel as if you're stuck in a traffic jam on Lake Shore Drive. At least the trains in Chicago are either on elevated tracks or are Metra trains that are short and fast. I'm starting to understand why those rural idiots drive around the flashing gate arms to play beat the train. The guy in front of me gets out of his pickup to rearrange the cord of firewood stacked in the bed of his truck. I imagine he feels more productive than me.

As the last boxcar comes into view down the track, my cell phone vibrates in my pocket. I always forget I have that thing. I quickly check my phone to see a new text message:

—My test yielded some interesting results—

Dammit, she's already seen her doctor. I was hoping to be there in case the results weren't good, and they must not have been, or else she would've used the word "good" instead of "interesting."

I shove my phone back in my pocket and start up my car. The guy in front of me gets back in the cab of his pickup just as the final freight car goes past. I can't remember the last time I saw a caboose on a train. The brake lights of the line of cars in front of me illumine as the gate arm begins to ascend. This feels like the start of the slowest NASCAR race ever.

The cars up ahead unhurriedly begin crossing the tracks. I consider passing as many of them as I can, but it seems as if the cars coming from the opposite direction are in more of a hurry, so the window of opportunity closes fast, if it was really ever open at all. A couple of cars way at the back of the line honk their horns. I consider joining in but resist the urge, as the discordant noise is clearly having no impact on the pace of our parade's progress.

Finally, after crossing the tracks, I'm able to break away from the slow slithering snake of vehicles onto a side road. I zigzag my way through neighborhoods to the doctor's office and pull into the small parking lot a bit too hot, squeaking my brakes as I come to a stop in an open spot near the door. I live about five miles away, and it's taken me thirty minutes to get here. I hop out of my car and look around for Rebecca's Jeep, hoping she hasn't left already.

I don't see her Jeep anywhere. I check my phone again in case I missed a call—no voicemails or new texts. I open the last text message I received and realize that it wasn't from Rebecca. Just then I spot Rebecca's Jeep pulling into the parking lot. She parks next to my car and quickly gets out, looking as harried as I feel.

"Sorry I'm late," she says. "I got held up by a train."

"That's okay." I open the door to the office for her.

"I would've called, but my phone died. You must've been waiting for like ever."

"Well, the important thing is that you're here now."

Chapter 16

I'm sitting on a plastic chair in the corner of the small, windowless room as Rebecca sits on the examination table. The nurse who showed us to the room assured us that the doctor would be with us momentarily. That was a lot of moments ago. It went completely unnoticed by the receptionist who checked us in that we were twenty minutes late for Rebecca's appointment. Apparently small-town doctors are as overscheduled as their counterparts in the city. I shift in a vain effort to make myself more comfortable on the cushionless seat. Rebecca dangles her legs off the end of the table and the paper she's sitting on makes a crinkling noise.

"Do you always have to wait so long to see your physician?"

"Not always, but it was a last-minute appointment, so I'm lucky that she could squeeze me in."

"If this is being squeezed, I'd hate to be stretched."

"I'm surprised that wait times where you used to live were shorter."

"They weren't, but I figured that these townie physicians doubled as animal doctors, so I thought they'd give top priority to their human patients."

"You came with me to be supportive, remember?"

"I am…I'm advocating that your healthcare needs should come before that of a chicken or a cow."

Considering the circumstances, I thought I was being rather droll, but I can tell from her expression that she thinks otherwise. "Sorry, all this waiting just reminds me of waiting for you at the emergency room…and I know as little now as I did then."

"Whatever this turns out to be, I'm glad you're here with me." She looks down at me from the edge of the exam table. "Now please stop talking."

There's a knock on the door, but before either of us can answer, the doctor enters the tiny room as if she's been blown in by a tornado.

"Sorry to keep you waiting," she says without bothering to look up from the manila folder in her hands.

"Are you really sorry," I ask, "or is that just how you begin all your appointments?"

"A few minutes ago, I had to send a patient of mine who had come in to see me about light-headedness and shortness of breath to the hospital for a myocardial infarction…you know, a heart attack. To make matters worse, the ambulance was delayed by a train."

"Well, I do hope this appointment goes better than that one," I say, feeling like a horse's ass. It suddenly occurs to me that I'm not sure if that idiom means a horse's buttocks, which I can't imagine would ever feel particularly bad since horses don't sit the way we do— and so that part of their bodies wouldn't get sore like our cans can—or a donkey owned by a horse, which might feel bad since it was owned not by a human that walked upright but rather by an animal that, for all intents and purposes, is just a larger version of itself…the way I might feel if I were owned by André the Giant, though I imagine he'd be a benevolent master. Yes, when referring to a diminished ego, I believe a horse's donkey makes more sense than a horse's posterior, but maybe I should ask the animal doctor for a second opinion...or perhaps I should just focus up. I tend to be a distraction to myself when I'm feeling anxious.

The doctor looks up from the folder. "I see, Ms. Hernandez, that you've decided to bring a visitor with you today."

"Yes, this is my boyfriend, and he's been very supportive and promises to be on his best behavior...from here on out."

"I have the results from your blood test. Are you sure you want me to share them—"

"Whatever it is, he deserves to know too. He's been as worried as I have...even more so, really. So is it just abdominal distress like the ER doctor thought?"

"Yes and no," the doctor answers as if that's any sort of answer at all.

"I get what you're trying to do," I blurt out without thinking. "You're closing up ranks to defend a woefully incompetent doctor rather than admitting that the initial diagnosis was mishandled...need I remind you that you took the Hippocratic Oath—not the Hypocrite Oath. Do you have any idea how little confidence I have in this backward community's ability to administer healthcare? If I were you, I'd be embarrassed to be a part of the local medical system, but it's fine if you're not because I'm plenty embarrassed for you."

"I suppose now would be a bad time to ask you to sign the copy of *Sawbones Spinster* that I keep at my desk."

"I'll dedicate my next book to you if you can just tell us what's wrong with my Becca."

"Your Becca had a bout of morning sickness."

Chapter 17

I'm driving us in a car…I think it's mine. I have no idea where we're going. I feel like the world's oldest teenager who just found out his girlfriend is pregnant.

"Since when am I your 'Becca'?"

"I don't know…since I found out my Becca is going to have our baby."

"What makes you think I'm going to keep it?"

"You don't want to?"

"I'd get rid of you before I got rid of it," Becca informs me. "I was just curious why you assumed I would keep it."

"I hope you'll keep both of us."

"That's good to know."

"I still don't understand how you got morning sickness at night."

"They just call it that. What I don't understand is why I didn't get morning sickness with either of my boys, but I'm getting it now."

"Every pregnancy is different." I'm trying to sound like I know something, but really I'm just parroting what the doctor told us.

"I know every pregnancy is different. I was there when the doctor said that, and I'm a woman who's been pregnant…twice."

"Then what don't you understand?" I make a sharp turn.

"They say that morning sickness can be tied to gender."

"Are 'they' the same people who call it morning sickness? Because 'they' don't really sound like geniuses."

"I wonder if this one will be a girl," she says to herself, not paying any attention to me at all—good for her.

"You know those people who tell you, 'We don't care if it's a boy or girl, so long as it's healthy'? What fools—I'd take a sickly girl over a healthy boy any day."

"You'd rather have a girl than a boy?"

"Well…I like your boys…or at least half of them…but if I had my druthers…though gender shouldn't really matter…so long as the baby is hale and hearty…why, what sort of family do you envisage?"

"Why can't you just say 'envision' like everybody else…and also, where are we going?"

"Where do you think we're going?" I ask earnestly. "Where would you like us to be going?"

"No, I mean, where are you driving us? I have to get back to work."

Chapter 18

My Becca needs a night to talk with her boys and to think things over. I know how she feels, but somehow I don't quite know how I feel. When I turned forty with no prospects (or desire) for marriage, I figured my chances of having a kid were minimal, and I was fine with that. When I turned fifty, nothing had changed; it just felt like forty plus. Now, at fifty-one, everything feels different and new.

I park in front of the KEEP OUT sign to check in with Edwin. I find him in the same spot I saw him last, staring down through a peephole at the vastness of the heavens above.

"Do you ever switch eyes?" I ask as I approach.

Edwin looks up from his telescope without looking at me. "No, but an old astronomy instructor of mine used to wear an eyepatch so that he didn't overtax his orbicularis oculi muscle. We called him the Pirate Professor."

"Great story...you got anything to drink?"

"Just flat cola and well water...I wouldn't recommend either." Ed studies me for a moment. "You seem like you're in a mood. Anything the matter?"

"Since when can you read people?"

"It's easy. I just need to know the person I'm reading for four decades. So what's up?"

"It's been an odd day is all."

"I think I'm about to make it odder still. That vitamin capsule you gave me turned out to be rather interesting."

"Was it filled with some kind of exotic substance?"

"Yes and no."

"You're the second person today who I've heard answer a question that way."

"The 'no' is that the ingredients are corn based," Ed continues, ignoring my comment, which he sometimes does. It's part of his condition; he ignores things people say when he doesn't know how to interpret them.

"Is that unusual?"

"Again, yes and no. Corn is rich in vitamin B constituents, such as thiamin and niacin, and minerals, such as phosphorus, magnesium, zinc, and selenium, as well as beta-carotene."

"I recognize those terms from the label on the multivitamin I take."

"Right, that's what got me curious. While all those things are found in corn, the manufacturer must've gone to considerable trouble to isolate them and then put them in those capsules."

"Why wouldn't they just buy their vitamins from a pharmacy?"

"Why not indeed, which brings us back to my 'yes' response to your exotic substance question."

"Corn isn't an exotic substance," I say. "Around here it's more common than concrete."

"True, but the way the corn has been manipulated is fascinating. I couldn't fully analyze the capsule's contents in my makeshift lab here, so I took it to campus and had a grad student run some 'testicles' as he put it…nice kid—let me use his mobile phone to text you."

"What did he find?"

"Beyond the prosaic vitamins and minerals I found, the capsule is laced with some designer compounds—really state-of-the-art stuff using phytochemicals."

"So what does that mean?"

"I'm not sure."

"I think I could get more of those capsules if that would help." I don't want to lose this lead.

"The tests the grad student ran involved an electron microscope, so trust me 'more' is not the issue."

"Then what is?"

"The issue is that those exotic compounds are so miniscule that they're effectively inert…they would likely either pass harmlessly through the human body, not unlike a kernel of corn in the digestive system, or simply get lost in all the chemical chaos."

"Then why would anyone go through all the trouble to put them there?"

"That's a good question," Ed tells me. "Which I'm afraid means I don't have a good answer for you."

"Then how do we find out?"

"It would help to have a look at the lab where the capsules were created."

"How do we do that?" I ask.

"I don't know. You're the one playing detective."

"Could the lab actually be located at the Big Farm?"

"It could be, but why would it be?" It makes me crazy when people answer a question with a question. "Like you said, corn is a commodity that isn't hard to come by."

"But what if these capsules are illegal?"

"They're not toxic, so why would they be illegal?"

"Have they been approved by the Food and Drug Administration?"

"Vitamins don't require FDA approval," Ed informs me.

"This really is odd."

"I told you."

"I could use a drink even more now...you've only got flat cola, huh?"

"Or well water."

"Man, I hate that stuff. My granddad had well water—tasted terrible...the iron turned all his white shirts brown in the wash." An inchoate idea begins to take shape in my head. "Do you think Dr. Weize could be the maker of these capsules?"

"I doubt it. I asked around about him while I was on campus. If he had a background in advanced chemistry, someone would've mentioned it. In fact, the only interesting thing I did hear was that before he went into academia, he was a co-developer of a cold-turkey, tough-love sort of program for addicts that proved unsuccessful; a couple of patients actually died during treatment, and the research that the program's philosophy was based on has since been discredited...but all that happened years ago, and he's had an unblemished career as a professor ever since."

"But you yourself said that everything is chemistry."

"I did say that, though I'm not sure why you're saying it now."

"Stamps."

"I'm familiar with them."

"You hold them and they're dry," I say. "You lick them and they get sticky."

"That is my understanding as well, though these days you buy them on sheets and they're already sticky...or of course, you could simply use electronic mail."

"Dr. Weize is a stamp collector...I could tell by the way he hovered over his collection that he's fanatical about them. Maybe he isn't involved in the chemistry part, but perhaps he cooked up the initial idea. The Big Farm has a well they use for their drinking water; the well water around here has iron in it. Similar to the way the properties of a stamp change when it's exposed to moisture, could the iron in the water cause a chemical reaction with the contents of the capsule the way it does in our blood and on the surface of Mars—the kind that spreads like rust on a car or cancer in the body?"

"The iron could, theoretically, behave as an activating agent," Ed replies, "but then how would they know if their patients are actually taking the vitamins?"

"The Big Farm's patients are required to undergo frequent drug tests."

"They could track consumption through urine analyses with a chemical marker and set up their very own double-blind experiment since the patients wouldn't know they were taking anything more than vitamins and the testers wouldn't know who was taking them until their experiment was concluded. All they would need to do to determine the efficacy of whatever they're testing is to compare the results of the urine analyses from the drug screenings with the outcomes of the patients."

"What could they be testing?" I ask.

"It could be anything, but the only reason to conduct an experiment as clandestinely as that is if they have a very good reason to keep whatever they're testing a secret."

"And if their operation truly is nefarious, then the lab might really be on the Farm so that they could oversee it."

"A small town is a good place to hide something that you don't want found."

"We need to have a look at that lab," I say.

"Now you're starting to sound like an actual detective."

Chapter 19

I've been driving around for an hour, thinking about Becca and the baby, as well as Sloan and the McCormick family. I can't imagine being the father of a child, but even harder to envisage is having a child who grows into an adult and then goes out into the flawed, wide world. What could possibly prepare a parent for that?

The third time I drive past Becca's house, I decide to stop. The boys must be asleep by now. If Becca is in a similar state of mind, she's probably going around in circles in her head like I am in my car. I slowly pull into her gravel driveway with my headlights off. As I get out, I pick up a few small rocks.

The house is dark. As noiselessly as I can, I walk toward the side of the house where Becca's bedroom window is located, but as I pass by the front door, I set off the motion-activated porch light. I freeze for a moment but don't see any lights come on inside. I'm not sure what I would do if they did. It's not like I could run back to my car and drive off undetected.

I position myself under her window and throw the first rock. It hits the siding a foot below the bottom of the window. It's difficult to aim in the dark. Now I wish the front porch light would come back on to provide a little illumination from around the corner. I try again, and this time I hit the soffit above the window. I try a third time and make contact with the windowpane.

One more ought to get her attention, but before I attempt my final throw, something in my pocket shakes…right, my cell phone that I always forget about.

"Hello," I whisper into the phone.

"Why are you throwing rocks at my house?" Becca asks.

"I was trying to be romantic."

"By behaving like a prowler?"

"Did I wake you?"

"Of course not, I've been staring at the ceiling for the last two hours."

"What were you thinking about?"

"Baby names."

"I like the name Verb. It works for either a boy or a girl, and when the kiddo explains to the teacher on the first day of school that the name Verb is actually a noun—automatic A."

"That's the dumbest thing I've ever heard. I'll meet you down on the front porch."

I hang up and walk back to the porch. I climb the three steps and take a seat on the porch swing. The thin, rusty chains protest my weight. Becca comes out in sweatpants and her bathrobe. She's never looked lovelier. "Care to sit down?"

"That swing only holds two."

"I don't think the baby is as heavy as all that yet."

She sits next to me, and the chains keen metallically again. I glance up at the hooks that hold the chains; they appear sturdy enough. "How are you feeling?"

"A mix of terrified and frightened."

"Frighterrified…that's understandable."

"Also a little excited…maybe a lot excited."

"Did you talk to the boys yet?"

"Vaguely."

"Is there anything I can do to help?"

"I made an appointment with an ob-gyn tomorrow after work. Could you pick up the boys from school?"

"Of course…is there anything else I can do?"

"Hold me."

Chapter 20

I stop by the mayor's office before lunch, but when I enter, I'm not sure if I'm in the correct store. There's no receptionist in the outer office, and the place looks like a sty, with papers strewn about as if they'd been used for confetti. I walk back to see if the mayor is in. I push through the half-open door to find the mayor asleep with his head on his desk. I exit, pulling the door shut behind me, and then loudly knock.

"Come in." I reenter the mayor's office as he straightens his tie. Three-day-old stubble covers his face, and his eyes are bloodshot. He wasn't asleep; he was passed out.

"I didn't see your receptionist out front." I sit down.

"I gave her the week off." The mayor drinks from a Styrofoam cup and then grimaces.

"Your office looks a bit unkempt...so do you, for that matter."

"Yeah, I've been trying to get caught up on some paperwork." He sees that I'm not buying it. "Truth be told, I've been trying to bury myself in work to keep from thinking about my son, and it's going about as well as it looks."

"Why don't you go home? I'm sure your wife is going through hell too. I can't imagine what either of you must be feeling."

"We're not close anymore...haven't been for a long time."

"Maybe you could be there for each other now."

"Maybe." The mayor wipes dried saliva off his cheek with the back of his hand and appears surprised to feel coarse stubble. "I'll give it some thought, but I don't think you came down here to play marriage counselor. Did you find out anything?"

"I'm pursuing a lead, as they say in the movies, but I could use some help."

"Sure...what do you need?"

"A warrant to search the grounds of the Big Farm and some men to help me conduct my search."

The mayor sits up in his chair. "Whoa...that's not a small request. First of all, mayors don't grant search warrants...I'm not even sure which judge I'd have to contact to have a search warrant issued for out there. Second of all, what happened to keeping this thing quiet? I thought you were just going to ask some casual questions."

"I did, but the answers I got led to more questions."

"What are you looking to find on the Farm?"

"An underground laboratory."

"Do you mean that literally or figuratively?"

"Possibly both," I answer.

"Why don't you ask your shooting buddy about it?"

"Because I think he might be involved. If he is, and I tip my hand by asking too many questions, he'll deny everything and then maybe relocate the lab."

The mayor opens his bottom desk drawer and rifles through it. He comes up with an eyedropper. Leaning back in his chair, he puts a drop of solution into each eye and then blinks hard.

Then the mayor says as he meets my gaze, "Okay, I don't want to do anything official, but that doesn't mean you can't still have a look-see. Go on out to our local airport at dusk to meet a pilot I know."

"At dusk? No, we need to sweep the grounds during the day, not flyover at night."

"Trust me...I've got it all worked out."

"When exactly did you work it out...while you were trying not to look hungover?" The mayor just stares at me. "Fine, so how will I find this pilot?"

"After five o'clock that airport is about as empty as a church on Saturday night...you won't have any trouble finding each other."

Chapter 21

Vance gets out of school first. I park my car in the pick-up queue in front of the high school. There are teenagers everywhere—pushing, cursing, flirting, laughing...the worst. Someday these idiots will be running the country...probably into the ground, though by then I'll likely be dead or warehoused, so it won't really matter much to me.

Over the next several minutes, herds of juveniles pile into the SUVs and minivans parked in front of me, and the line of vehicles begins to disperse—but still no Vance. The high school campus has mostly cleared of adolescents. Maybe Becca forgot to tell Vance this morning that I'd be picking him up, or maybe he gave me the slip. Either way, I figure he's found his own ride home by now.

As I start up my car, the back door opens. Vance climbs into the backseat, slams the door, and orders me to "drive."

"I'm not your damn chauffeur," I say over my shoulder. "Come sit up here in the passenger's seat."

"Why?"

"Because if we get into a head-on collision, there's a better chance of you getting thrown through the windshield."

Vance grumpily gets out of the backseat and grouchily gets into the front seat, slamming the door each time.

I pull away from the curb. "How was school today?"

"Ticky tack, wicky whack."

"Sounds like you're doing well in your English class."

"School blows."

"That's funny, I had the opposite opinion when I was your age. I thought school sucked."

"Talked to my moms last night."

"All of them, or just the one I know?"

"Sounds like I'm going to be stuck seeing more of you from now on."

"I doubt it...I don't plan to visit you at boarding school." Vance gives me a look that makes me hope the students have to pass through metal detectors at the high school. "Easy—it was just a joke...I'll visit when I can."

"Moms is always saying how you got a sense of humor...she never said nothing about it being defective."

"Have you found in your young life that people respond well to unsolicited criticism?"

"Whatevs."

"Good point," I concede. "You're done with school kind of early, aren't you?"

"What are you even talking about? We're in school mad late this year because of all the snow days we had over winter."

"No, I mean don't you do any after-school stuff…you know, extracurricular activities like sports or clubs."

"I'm not really into that scene."

"Do you work after school then?"

"I ain't got no job…I don't get my license until next year."

"You could get a paper route," I suggest. "With all that's going on in the world these days, I bet newspapers are selling like hotcakes."

"I don't know what either of those things are."

"And this whole time I thought you weren't funny. So then what do you do with all your free time—hit the books?"

"Mostly pick my nose…I like to use the pointy end of my toothbrush."

"That's a coincidence," I say. "I like to use the pointy end of your toothbrush to pick my nose too. So besides having booger-free nostrils, what are your plans for the future?"

Vance stares out the window at a cornfield. I should've known he wouldn't answer such a direct question, but then to my surprise, he does.

"I want to study civil engineering at the university."

"Good school…tough major. How are your grades?"

"Crappy." The boy looks at me with a morose expression, and then he returns to staring out the window. This isn't going well. I pull my car over. "What are you doing?"

"There's only one high school in this town, but from what I understand, there are about a half dozen elementary schools, and I'm not exactly sure where your brother's is located, so do you mind driving us there?"

Vance is momentarily stunned. I'm a little surprised by my request too, even though I'm the one who made it.

"You're going to let me drive your car?"

"As long as you don't drive it into a ditch."

We get out and trade seats. I've never sat on the passenger's side of my car before—feels weird. Vance adjusts the mirrors, and then the driver's seat, and then the mirrors again.

"You know how to drive, right?" I ask, wondering if I'll live to regret this. "I mean at least a little."

"Sure, I've played Grand Theft Auto."

"Oh good, I was worried there for a moment."

He puts the car into drive and slowly pulls us back onto the rural road. He's white-knuckle driving at ten miles under the speed limit.

"I like the way this car rides." He keeps his hands at exactly ten and two. "They don't make them like this anymore."

"Everybody likes these vintage cars until it comes time to have them repaired; then only overpriced mechanics like them."

For his first time driving, Vance does a very mediocre job, but I only have to grab the steering wheel once in a moment of heart-stopping panic when he overcorrects after executing a wide turn. My pulse returns to a less than cardiac-arrest-is-imminent level. "We're getting back into a residential area, so why don't you pull over, and I'll take over...but nice work."

Vance pulls the car onto the shoulder, and we switch seats again. I resume driving duty, and soon we're parking in front of Lance's school. I recognize some of the SUVs and minivans in the pick-up queue from the high school, though maybe they just look the same.

Van breaks the silence first as we wait for Lance to come out. "Yo, thanks for letting me take your whip for a spin."

"I know it's not easy being your age, so once in a while, it's good to let off some steam and just go for a drive, though driving was more stressful when I was a teenager, since we had to dodge all those dinosaurs."

The bell rings inside the school, and within moments a hundred or so little kids come bounding out of the doors. Lance races to the car and hops into the backseat.

"Hey, Van! Hey, Wes-two thousand-pounds!"

"I've got to tell you kiddo—that one's not my favorite."

Chapter 22

The airport consists mostly of chain-link fences and corrugated metal hangars that only look large enough to house the smallest of airplanes. I hate flying in tiny prop planes. I walk along the perimeter fence until I find an unlocked gate adjacent to a hangar with a wide-open bay door. I look inside the hangar, but I only see a couple of small aircraft—no people.

"Hello." My voice echoes off the thin walls.

"Who are you helloing for?" someone behind me asks. I turn to see Officer Slim holding a can of oil.

"Dammit, huckleberry, you startled me."

"Didn't mean to spook you, tough guy."

"You seem to be everywhere in this town. I figured a guy that looks like you would spend most of your time hiding under a bridge or a rock. So what are you doing here...helping out by performing menial chores...manual labor...scut work and such...fetching things...sweeping up...please tell me you're not the pilot."

"Yep, I am."

"Double dammit...I thought you good old boys just drove tractors."

"I've been flying since before I could drive," Slim informs me. "My daddy was an airman back in 'Nam."

"Then is he available?"

"You're stuck with me, sport." Slim opens the hood to the engine compartment of the plane nearest the bay door. "Hop on in. I'm just going to top off the oil."

I climb into the side-by-side two-seater. I've sat in bathtubs larger than this cockpit. Slim closes the hood and then somehow folds his tall frame into the seat next to me.

"Cozy…what kind of plane is this?"

"A Cessna 150—a true classic. I overhauled the engine myself."

"And it leaks oil?"

"She runs like a dream."

"Well, this is starting to feel like a nightmare."

"Here, put this on." He hands me a headset. "I'm going to start up the engine, so it'll get noisy. Just speak into the microphone if you want to say something, but—you know—don't feel like you have to or anything."

Slim pops open the small window in his door and shouts, "Clear!" Then the propeller springs to life.

"Who the hell are you yelling at?" I ask into my headset's mic. "We're the only ones here."

"Oh, did they teach the start-up procedure different where you got your pilot's license?"

"I don't have a pilot's license."

"Then buckle up and shut up."

We slowly taxi out of the hangar and onto the most potholed runway I've ever seen. Slim revs the engine.

"You know, I read one of your books before— *Skywriting Spinster*."

"Great, I can hardly wait to hear what you didn't like about it."

"I thought it was too talky."

And with that we accelerate down the runway as fast as the little plane will carry us, taking off and just clearing the perimeter fence.

Chapter 23

We've been flying for fifteen minutes. The ground below, at least what I can see of it on this overcast night, looks so different from up here. The roads seem longer, the lakes seem bigger, and once we fly past the town, the patchwork of rectangular cropland extends in every direction.

"All these farms look the same," I say into the mic. "How will we find the Big Farm...especially now that it's almost dark?"

"We'll use GPS genius." Slim holds up a Garmin handheld.

"Oh, I thought that was your cell phone."

"Okay, we're getting close. Grab that case behind the seats. It's got a thermal imaging camera inside."

I practically pull my back out trying to get the heavy case over the seats, but finally I'm able to wrestle it into my lap. I open the case and pull out a device that looks like a high-tech camcorder. "Now I understand. We're doing this in the dark so that we pick up more contrast between warm-blooded people and the ground, which is cooler at nighttime."

"No, we're doing this in the dark so they don't see us. The sun just set, so the ground hasn't cooled all that much...besides these things work about as well during the day as they do at night. I thought you were supposed to be smart."

"My bailiwick is more identifying irony...things of that nature."

"Well, ain't that all kinds of helpful right about now."

I try to turn the camera on. "How did your Podunk department ever afford this equipment?"

"We didn't. It's more or less on permanent loan from Chicago PD. We borrowed it to find an underground meth lab that was supplying a Southside gang...or whatever the politically correct term is nowadays."

"Did it work?"

"Sure, we found the lab and shut down the operation, but these days most of the meth heads just cook in their vehicles."

"That sounds frustrating."

"That's police work for you. Bust one bad guy and two more take his place, but if you don't catch the first one, then you'd end up with three."

I fiddle with the camera a bit more until I get it to work. The small LCD screen shows mostly blues and purples with some splotches of oranges and reds mixed in. "I think we're in business."

"All right then, I'll take us down and do a few passes above the Farm."

Slim steers the airplane into a slow descent. We fly back and forth over the Big Farm several times. I see orange, people-shaped figures in the farmhouse, the machine shed, and the barracks...all right where they should be. "Nobody seems to be out of place down there."

"What about by the creek?" Slim asks. "I thought I saw some orange on the screen when we flew out that way."

"No, those were inmates too. Some of them like to camp by the creek. Anyway, they wouldn't set up a lab that close to water. If it was underground, the water might seep in, and if it was above ground, they'd run the risk of getting flooded out during a heavy rain."

"Good point. I guess that means we struck out."

"I think it's still a full count. The shooting club isn't too far from here. Do you think you can find it?"

"Yes, I believe I can."

Slim flies us northwest for ten minutes, consulting his GPS device a couple of times. With all the noise the engine is making, it seems like we should be moving faster, but our airspeed feels slower than I sometimes drive on empty stretches of Interstate.

"Okay, it should be below us," Slim announces, "give or take."

I watch the camera's screen as we fly over the main house. Plenty of oranges and reds inside, and outside only blues and purples.

"Fly over that way a bit." I point in the direction of the shooting range. I aim the camera toward the range, and suddenly a dozen or so orange figures show on the screen. "I think we've got something."

"What is that over there?" Slim asks.

"A skeet shooting range."

"How do you know they're not just out shooting clay pigeons then?"

"At night?" I ask.

"Maybe they've got night-vision goggles. Some of those gun nuts can get pretty deep into playing soldier."

"Or maybe they're underground. I can't tell on this tiny screen, and with the cloud cover, I can't eyeball it either."

"Then we'll have to find out if they're topside or not."

"How do you propose we do that?" As if to answer my question, Slim banks into a steep descent. I pitch forward, but the seat belt keeps me from hitting the windshield. "You're not going to try to land here, are you?"

"Nope, my plan is to do a low flyover and buzz them—just keep an eye on the screen to see if we run 'em off."

"Your plan is to scare people with guns who might be wearing night-vision goggles?"

"I never said it was a good plan."

We hurtle toward the ground at a velocity I didn't think this old heap could muster, though I suppose gravity is doing most of the work. As we take on speed, the plane makes unholy noises that seem to portend obliteration. Just when it feels as if we're definitely going to crash, Slim levels out, and the plane begins to climb again.

"Did those sons of bitches scatter?"

"They didn't budge at all," I answer with a grin. "Gotcha."

Chapter 24

From the mayor's office, Slim and McCormick spend the rest of the night making phone calls to help secure a search warrant for the county sheriff. They coordinate with her department and devise a plan to execute the warrant at dawn. Fearing a reenactment of the Waco siege, the sheriff is reluctant to march onto the premises of a shooting club, catching them unawares first thing in the morning, with less than a full complement of deputies, so she makes her own calls to get officers to come in on their days off and even reactivates a couple of recently retired deputies to fill out her hunting party.

Slim left an hour ago to join up with the sheriff's posse as a liaison for the township, though he won't have any official jurisdiction. While we wait for Slim to report back, the mayor and I watch the sunrise through the venetian blinds of the office's storefront window and drink cold coffee. The sleepless night hasn't done either of us any good.

"Do you have any kids?" the mayor asks.

"Not as of yet, though lately I've been thinking that having a family seems like a pretty good idea."

"It is…though starting at your age might be a challenge, but then what part of parenthood isn't challenging?"

"Do you worry about your kids more when they're young or when they get older?"

"Of course you're always concerned, but Sloan had so many health issues as a little kid that his mother and I would worry night and day over him, but then we—well, the doctors really—figured out that his health problems were caused by food allergies. Once we changed his diet, he became a healthy little boy and grew into a strong young man, so I thought we were free and clear. Maybe I let my guard down too much."

"How can you ever know a hundred percent?" I'm not even sure what I'm asking, but thankfully the mayor regards my question as rhetorical. "What was Sloan allergic too?"

"Just about everything they serve in a school lunch: dairy, peanuts, corn."

"He was allergic to corn?"

"Yeah, he had a severe corn allergy."

"Was that a cause for concern?" I ask. "You know, him working on a farm where they grow corn?"

"Not really. Sloan had gotten pretty good about monitoring his diet over the years, and he always kept an EpiPen on him. Besides, all they grow out there is feed corn, which is what most of the farms around here plant."

"So I've come to learn."

"What is it that you think they're going to find in that lab anyhow? With all the hullabaloo about locating this secret lab, I never stopped to ask what you think it's being used for."

"There is no lab." Slim enters the office like a cold gust of wind.

"How could you not find it?" I ask in disbelief. "You knew right where to look."

"No, we found 'it.' " Slim sits down and stretches his long legs out in front of him. " 'It' just wasn't a lab."

The mayor sits up straight. "What was it then?"

"An underground shooting range. They denied it was there at first, but when we threatened to find it ourselves, bringing in excavation equipment if necessary, they showed us the entrance out in the woods. They had a big cache of guns down there, including some illegal firearms like a tommy gun that the sheriff confiscated, but since nobody was down there at the time, we didn't make any arrests...the club will probably just end up being fined."

"A fine?" asks the mayor.

"There was no back room where a lab might've been?" I ask.

"Most of it was just an open space where they had targets set up...real elaborate stuff with mannequins wearing fatigues, popping out of doorways. Look, I know you wanted this one...we gave it a hell of a try, but like I told you, those gun nuts can get pretty deep into playing soldier."

"All that for a fine," the mayor says, "which will end up going to the county."

"I'm sorry I got your hopes up," I reply. "I thought...I don't know what I thought."

The mayor looks at me with eyes that have not known restful sleep for days. "You thought you were doing some good. As the officer said, you tried, and I appreciate that."

Slim stands up. "Let's not get too down in the mouth about this. We did manage to seize some illegal guns that could've made their way into to the wrong hands—all in all, not a bad morning's work. But…I promised my boy to take him squirrel hunting today, so I'm going to get."

"I think I'll be going too." I slink toward the door with Slim. "Mr. Mayor, maybe you should go home and get some sleep."

Chapter 25

I drive out to Edwin's place to update him on the search for the lab, but really I'm hoping that my oldest friend will commiserate with me on my failure, though he's not too proficient at the emotional stuff. The night owl might still be sleeping, which is what I should be doing, but I feel more beaten than tired and need to go somewhere besides home.

It's easier to sneak up on Edwin in the daytime than at night, since there are no headlights to be seen through the trees. I find him hanging wet clothes on a line suspended between a hook on the housing of the radar dish and a fence post. It never occurred to me that he does his laundry out here. I step out of the woods. "Good morning."

"Jumping beans!" Ed spins around, dropping a wet pair of jeans in the process. "You gave me a start."

"I thought you could hear my footsteps."

"Only when I know to listen for them."

"I wasn't sure you'd be up this early."

"I haven't gone to sleep yet." Ed picks up the fallen pair of pants and hangs them on the line. "In the summertime I usually sleep in the afternoons to stay out of the heat. So what brings you out here this morning?"

"I came to update you on the search for the lab. At dawn the county sheriff executed a search warrant. I guess you can tell from my expression how it went."

"From what I've come to understand, interpreting expressions has a lot to do with noticing slight variances in the dilation of the pupils and the contraction of the muscles around the eyes—we're talking about fractions of an inch. I spend most of my time observing celestial bodies that are many light years apart."

"I see your point, so I'll spare you the suspense…it did not go well."

"They didn't find the lab?"

"No, and I also learned that the young man who died had a severe corn allergy. Could those vitamins have sent him into anaphylactic shock?"

"Possibly, if he took enough of them and his allergy was acute…or his allergic reaction could've exacerbated, perhaps even altered, the effects of the phytochemicals."

"He probably had an EpiPen," I add. "Could epinephrine have affected the phytochemicals?"

"Adrenaline…sure, that could potentially disrupt a chemical reaction in the body. With all that might've been going on in his system, there's any number of catastrophic conditions that could've developed."

"So then what should we do? Can we send the sample somewhere to be studied further?"

"We could, but without knowing how the phytochemicals were developed or even what their intended purpose is, the compounds would essentially have to be reverse engineered in order to be fully assayed, and then a battery of tests would need to be performed to mimic the complex chemical processes of human physiology. You're looking at thousands of lab technician hours…all for something that we don't know is any more sinister than secretly testing a new, cutting-edge nutritional supplement."

"You think I might be looking for a villain, like in one of my books, where none exists?"

"I think if you were, it would be understandable...and forgivable."

"Maybe I am trying to connect dots that don't connect, and there are probably even more dots that I'm not seeing. Perhaps I should return to my writing so that I can revise the story when it's not to my liking. Besides, the McCormick family needs rest and time to heal...not more wild-goose chases. No matter what I might be able to turn up, it won't change the fact that their son is dead."

"I wish there was more I could do for you, my friend."

"There is one thing," I say. "A kid I know wants to attend your university after he graduates high school to study civil engineering. Any chance you could ask one of your contacts at the college to save him a spot?"

"That's a competitive program. How are his grades?"

"Not so good."

"Is he a minority of any kind?"

"His mother's part Hispanic and his father's a former drug addict."

"So what's that make the kid?"

"A pain-in-the-ass teenager."

"Hardly a minority there," Edwin says. "Get me his transcripts, and I'll see what I can do."

Part Two

Chapter 1

Holy hell, it's cold. It's a sunny afternoon, but the gusting winds have made my face numb, though not enough to keep me from feeling the water at the corner of my eyes freeze. Slim suggested we go ice fishing. I imagined a warm little shanty with comfortable seats. Instead we're sitting atop upturned buckets out in the open on a frozen, windswept lake. Man that guy's a dimwit. If I ever write him as a character in one of my books, I'll have to change his nickname to Dim...besides, Slim reminds me of a Jim Croce song.

"I have to see a man about a horse," I say. "Where should I go?"

"You told me you used to go fishing with your granddaddy, so you know the drill, go anywhere you want...just don't piss in the ice hole."

"You're an ice hole. You mean I have to walk all the way back to the bank to find a tree to pee on?"

"You don't have to—just go over there." Slim vaguely points behind him. "Trust me, I won't look."

"But we're on a lake. I already feel stupid enough out here in the open with no fish to show for our efforts. What if somebody happens to be passing by?"

"Then they'll get a little show—probably very little...only partially on account of the cold."

"Is it cold?" I stomp away. "I hadn't noticed."

I spot a dead tree sticking up through the ice a ways off, but it's still closer than the shoreline. I figure the tree will offer some privacy, at least in one direction, and I really need to go because of the beers I've drunk and, you know, being in my fifties. Slim had brought a warm case of Budweiser and set it right on the ice, assuring me that the cans would be cold in no time—great, maybe after this we can sit in a sauna and drink some hot toddies.

I make my way over to the tree, nearly slipping a couple of times. I take one last look around to make sure nobody is watching me from the bank…all clear. As I'm about to unzip and do my business, I hear a cracking sound under my feet. I instinctively start to back away, but it's too late. I'm in the icy water before I fully realize what's happened.

I bear hug the trunk and try to climb up, but the dead tree is wet and brittle. I stretch out for the ice shelf that's formed around the tree, but what I can reach with my fingertips collapses at the slightest pressure. My extremities feel heavy and useless. I briefly wonder if you can be aware that you're going into cold shock or if you're already there before you know it.

Slim must've heard all my flailing about, because out of nowhere he's thrown a rope for me to grab hold of.

"Grab hold of the rope!"

I wish I could keep my teeth from chattering long enough to berate him for his patently obvious instructions, but instead it takes all my effort to grip the rope, though I can't make my fingers close completely. Slim pulls on the rope, and it slips through my half-clenched fists. I see him looking around for something as my head bobs under. In my windpipe, I suddenly feel a cold sensation the likes of which I've never experienced. I'm jolted back into cognizance of my situation as I expectorate and start to tread water again.

Slim tosses the rope once more; this time there's a large stick tied to the end of it, which floats nearby.

"Grab the stick."

I do as instructed, throwing my arms over the stick and wrapping the rope around my wrists. Slim tugs on the rope, and I slowly slide out of the water onto the ice. After what feels like an hour of being dragged across the ice, Slim stops pulling and comes over to help me sit upright.

"How are you feeling?" He puts his coat over my shoulders.

"Well…I don't have to pee anymore."

"Go figure—a smart guy like you who doesn't know that you're not supposed to walk near things sticking up out of the ice…that's where it's the weakest. I believe this might be some of that irony you're so fond of."

Part of me wishes I'd died. The rest of me wishes that Slim had been the one to perish while attempting to rescue me—the towering oaf.

Chapter 2

Slim and I load up his truck with the fishing gear. "So why didn't you just holler for help?"

"I don't know," I say, still shivering. "I guess I didn't think of it."

"Everybody's got to ask for help sometimes."

"I hear you."

"Especially when you're up to your neck in it."

"I understand what you're telling me."

"There's no shame in needing a hand now and then."

"I get it."

"The only shame is being too proud to—"

"Can you please start up your truck and turn on the heater?" I open the passenger's side door. "See...me asking for help."

We drive the snowy roads back to town, and my shivers give way to a nauseous feeling. My skin is clammy and my forehead warm.

"You don't look so good," Slim observes.

"I've felt better."

"You know, taking an ice bath in the lake during the middle of winter is a good way to catch a cold."

"No...I didn't know that."

Slim fiddles with the radio, passing three songs that I like, before choosing the signoff jingle for a commercial that he practically sings along with. "No matter what kind of fish you're angling for when wearing your rubber waders/Remember you can always count on us because we're your local master baiters." Once the commercial reaches its conclusion, Slim says, "That's where I got the wax worms we were using."

"I still can't believe we were fishing out in the freezing cold, hoping to catch fish that consider larvae a delicacy."

"I've been going to that bait shop since I was a kid. I must've heard that little ditty just about every day for over thirty years now."

"I guess that radio spot must be what passes for wit around here."

"What do you mean?" Slim asks with a stone-faced expression.

"You know...'we're your local master baiters.' "

Slim looks at me, and I look back at him for a sign that he's putting me on, but I don't see a sign of anything.

"Come on, really?" I ask. "I'd spell it out for you, but I doubt you know how to read—master baiters...masturbators."

"I'm not sure what you're getting at. Must be some sort of big-city thing that hasn't made its way down here yet."

I shake my head, and just as I'm about to roll my eyes, I notice the corner of his mouth twist up into a grin.

"So where am I dropping you off...Becky's place?"

"Yeah, it feels as if I practically live there now—good thing I spent all that time fixing up my house."

"You could sell it, but then you'd probably have to take a big loss, since the housing market around here is in the tank."

"Aren't you just full of helpful information today? If you want, you're welcome to stay for dinner; we're ordering pizza."

"Thanks," Slim says, "but I'm picking up my boy from his mom's place. We're having venison tonight."

"Sounds scrumptious."

Chapter 3

It takes all the effort I can muster to climb the three front porch steps. I stumble in the front door and collapse onto the couch, still wearing my coat.

"You don't look so good," Lance says from the other end of the couch. I didn't even see him down there. "Did you catch any fish?"

"The only thing I caught was a cold." I notice that the television is on. "What're you watching?"

"A cartoon about this team of robots that fights crime, but when the bad guys are really bad, they come together to form a giant robot."

"If they're more effective at fighting crime as a giant robot, then why don't they just always stay that way?"

"I don't know," Lance replies.

"Maybe the robots don't feel as if they can express their individual personalities when they're part of the giant robot."

"Well...they're robots, so I don't think that's it, but it's a good show. I'm in the middle of a three-hour marathon. Do you want to watch it with me?"

"Of course, let the mind numbing recommence."

Becca enters the living room...or rather her very pregnant belly enters the living room with herself arriving a few minutes later.

"Oh, I didn't know you were back. You don't look so good."

"That seems to be the prevailing opinion."

"At least you only look like you feel under the weather. I feel like I'm ten months pregnant and look as big as a house."

"You're selling yourself short, my dear. You don't look as big as a house; you look as big as a mansion—with a billiards room…and an indoor pool."

She sits on me as punishment for my insolence. Then Van comes into the living room with a book and sulkily sits between us and Lance. If the occupants of this couch were cartoon robots, we could form a formidable giant robot indeed.

"How's the story you're reading Vancy?" Becca asks.

Van replies with a shrug of his shoulders, which qualifies as a fairly fulsome response from him.

"What are you reading?" I ask.

"*The Most Dangerous Game*." Van seems annoyed by all the questions.

"Ah, Richard Connell," I say. "That's a good one."

"It's okay," Van agrees-ish with me.

"I read that one back in high school too," adds the gravid landslide that I'm currently buried under.

"I don't really get the point of it," Van says. "I mean, it's an entertaining read and all, but my English teacher wants us to identify its theme…like what, that it's not okay to hunt people. I didn't need to read this story to understand that."

"It's been a few years since I was in high school," Becca says, "but isn't there some question about whether it's cruel to hunt animals—including humans—if they can reason…or if it's cruel to kill any animal that can feel fear?"

"What does that have to do with me?" Van asks. "I'm not a hunter."

"But you make choices that impact other animals," she answers.

"Like what?"

"Like whether you want pepperoni or mushroom on your pizza tonight," I add.

Becca's cell phone chimes from the kitchen, and she rises to answer it, putting her hand on my chest for support as she struggles to her feet, nearly collapsing my lungs in the process—glad to be of assistance.

"So it's about vegetarianism?" Van asks me as I gasp for breath.

"Maybe," I wheeze, "but if memory serves, wasn't there also some bit about the laws of a civilized society?"

"What do you mean?" Van asks.

"Well, I'm not exactly sure," I respond. "It's been ages since I've read it, and you're the one who's supposed to be figuring out what it means, but as I recall, General Zaroff was civilized in manner, except—"

"That he hunts people," Van says. "But he lives on his own island, so really he's created his own civilization where he alone makes the rules."

"And how does that work out for visitors to the island?" I ask.

"Not well at all," Van answers.

"Hey," Lance protests, "I'm trying to watch my show, and I was here first."

Becca returns to the living room with a concerned countenance. I look at her as if to ask what the matter is, and she hands me her cell phone.

"It's for you."

"Someone's trying to call me on your phone?"

"I think you should take it upstairs."

"I sense a complication coming on," I reply, taking the phone.

Chapter 4

I should've brought Kleenex with me. I've been snorting snot back into my nasal cavities for the last couple of hours because the bathroom at the police station doesn't have tissue, though it does have the world's thinnest, most pointless toilet paper—seemingly a blend of onionskin and cheesecloth. Just as I consider untucking my shirt and using it to give my nose a good blow, the desk sergeant informs me that Rodney Delacroix is being processed for release.

Another few minutes pass as I continue to wait on the metal bench, until finally I see a hulking corrections officer emerge from the doorway leading to the jail in the back of the building. He unlocks the security door, and then from behind him, a shamefaced Rodney appears. The officer undoes his handcuffs, and the desk sergeant has him sign a few forms. Then the sergeant empties a manila envelope containing Rodney's personal effects, which are a thin wallet, a cheap watch, and a few coins.

Rodney collects his things and walks over to me. "Thanks for bailing me out and for picking me up."

"Sure." I stand to greet him. A handshake feels out of place; maybe I should offer one of those fist bump things. Instead, I lightly pat him on the shoulder. "How are you feeling?"

"It's been a long day," Rodney answers dejectedly. "Did the sarge tell you what I was charged with?"

"I didn't ask."

"I got into a crash, driving a pickup that belongs to the Farm...it wasn't even my fault. Some old man ran a stop sign and turned in front of me."

"Then why did they arrest you?" I ask as we exit to the parking lot.

"The old-timer was pretty banged up, so he had to be taken to the hospital. The cops detained me, and because of my priors, they took a blood sample. I tested positive for opioids. I swear I've been clean since I got to the Big Farm."

"This is me." I unlock my car.

"Nice ride." Rodney opens the passenger's side door.

"Thanks, I've had it for years." I turn on the engine to warm up the car. "So do you think there was some kind of mistake with the test then?"

"Maybe, but I don't see how...as far as I know, I've passed all my drug screenings out at the Farm."

"Do you think the cops are trying to frame you?" I don't, but I want to get a sense of where Rodney's head is.

"I doubt it...they've always been straight with me before."

"So then where does that leave you?"

"It leaves me in violation of my parole, out of a job, homeless, and broke." Rodney shakes his head. "Listen, I don't mean to lay all this on you. I just didn't know who else to turn to. All my friends are either addicts or recovering addicts—none of who have any money. Becky's was the only number I could think to call, but I didn't want her coming down here, and you seemed like a decent guy when we met."

"I understand." I'm not sure I really do. "You mentioned broke. Haven't you been squirrelling away your earnings for the work you do on the Farm? It's not like you've been using it to pay Rebecca child support."

"Right…sorry about that. The Farm just gives us a stipend for incidental expenses like toiletries…a small fraction of the money we're owed. They don't pay us the rest until we complete the treatment program. They told us it limits our temptation and gives us something to work toward. Anyway, I thought I would be finished with the program by now."

"But you've been out there for a while." I try to do some quick math. "How much longer do you have in your program?"

"It's up to the doc. If he thinks you've made enough progress, then you're good to go."

"Then how long would you say most of the inmates stay patients out there?"

"Like I said, it all depends on when the doc tells you that you're better, but the few inmates I've known who've been released from the program usually spend as much time out there as their sentences would've been if they'd stayed in prison."

"That could amount to years of cheap labor from each inmate."

"True," Rodney replies, "but it still beats sitting in a cage most of the day, and you maybe get to make a little money—plus there's always a chance that you might get out sooner."

"But because of this one infraction, you're out of the program and might be facing more prison time?"

Something isn't adding up. "You must've passed countless drug screenings at the Farm. Do you think they might consider this test an anomaly?"

"They got a zero-tolerance policy. One positive and you're done…be it their drug tests or the law's."

"And you have no idea how these opioids got into your system?"

"I know it doesn't make any sense, but yeah…my blood should be as clean as a ninety-year-old nun's."

"So where are you going to stay?" I ask, realizing that my car is now rather warm. "Where am I driving you?"

"My parole violation hearing is next week, and I figure they'll book me a room at the gray bar hotel then." Rodney gives me a hangdog look. "Maybe I could sleep at Becky's place until then…on the couch, of course."

"I think that would be weird for the boys." Not to mention me.

"Then maybe you could lend me some money for a motel. There's a real cheap one just outside of town."

I briefly consider the suggestion, but the notion of a former addict—who's down on his luck and possibly facing a protracted prison sentence—staying in a seedy motel with nothing but unstructured time on his hands doesn't play well in my head, though the counterproposal I'm about to offer isn't without cause for trepidation.

"You can bunk at my granddad's old house."

Chapter 5

It's almost midnight by the time I get Rodney situated at my house and then back to Becca's place. Her house is dark, so I let myself in and quietly make my way up the stairs. I've done this enough times now that I know which steps are creaky and to be avoided, but near the top of the stairs, my stomach lets out a loud rumble. I consider going back downstairs to see if there's any leftover pizza in the kitchen but then reconsider; I'm more tired than hungry, and the sooner I get horizontal, the sooner my nose will stop running—hopefully. Besides, at my age, if I eat pizza—especially with pepperoni—right before I go to bed, I'll be awake for at least an hour, no matter how tired I am.

I steal into Becca's room, change for bed in the dark, and slip under the covers without waking her…or so I think.

"How did it go?"

"I didn't mean to wake you."

"It's okay…between the little girl kicking in my belly and your belly on the stairs, I haven't been able to sleep much tonight. There's pizza in the fridge."

"Pepperoni?" I ask.

"And mushroom. So what was Rod arrested for?"

"Drugs."

"Possession?"

"Not exactly...he was involved in a traffic accident, so they tested him and found opioids in his system, which—"

"Puts him in violation of his parole, which means he'll probably end up going back to prison—my boys' father, the felon."

"He swore he was clean though. Any chance that's true?"

"Almost every addict tells you that when they get caught relapsing."

"Right, but you know Rodney well...is there a chance that he could be telling the truth?"

"Yeah, I know Rod real well, so I know there's even less of a chance that he's telling the truth."

"But it sounds like you're saying there's still a slight chance?"

"What are you doing?" Becca asks.

"What do you mean?"

"I mean why do you think this person who you barely know, who you have no reason to like, might be innocent when everyone is telling you that he isn't?"

"A hunch—maybe. Something still doesn't add up for me about Sloan and the Big Farm."

"Trust me, when it comes to addicts, the math can be complicated. You tried to help Sloan's family...you did your best, but—"

"—but it wasn't enough," I interrupt to finish her sentence.

"No, what I was going to say, if you'd let me finish my own sentence, is that there was nothing to be done."

"I feel like I could've done more."

"I don't understand you...first you didn't want to do anything, but you did as much as anyone could expect, and now you're upset that it wasn't enough. The McCormick family appreciates what you did...maybe now your focus should be on our family."

"I like the sound of that." I drape my arm over her humungous belly.

After a moment of silence, I start to drift off to sleep, but then Becca asks, "Does Rod know that we're expecting?"

"He didn't ask about you, so I assume so."

"Where did you take him after you bailed him out?"

"To my house."

"You really are the patron saint of lost causes."

"That's impossible...I'm not even Catholic. Incidentally, which one is that?"

"St. Jude."

Chapter 6

Slim signals the waitress for more coffee. She eagerly comes over and refills his mug, winking at him as she loudly chews her gum. So many adults down here chew gum; I still don't get it. I practically have to clink my mug with his to get the waitress to notice that I could use a refill too. She tops me off while looking at someone coming through the entrance and then leaves our table before I have a chance to ask for the check.

"How was the venison last night?"

"Not bad," Slim answers. "We made a stew, which is about the only way I can get that boy to eat vegetables."

"Who would've thought that deer meat could encourage a kid to eat vegetables?"

"It always tastes better when you kill it yourself." Slim sips his coffee. "I saw the paperwork for yesterday's arrests when I got into work this morning. Looks like Becky's ex is in some trouble."

"Yeah, that's why I called to see if you had a few minutes to grab some coffee."

"I figured."

"Are you sure you don't want a doughnut or something?" I look around for the waitress. "I thought that was sort of a big thing with you guys."

"I had breakfast before I started my shift." Slim leans back in the booth. "So what's the ask?"

"What do you mean?"

"What I mean is that I know you called me because of Becky's ex, but what I don't know is what you're going to ask me to do about him. If you want me to get him out of this mess, it's too late because he's already been processed, and I wouldn't anyhow. If you want me to see to it that he goes away for a long time, that's not under my control, and I wouldn't anyhow."

"When I bailed him out of jail last night, he told me that he'd been clean for months—that there was no way drugs should've been in his system. Is there any chance—"

"None," Slim categorically answers. "We've never gotten a false-positive with the test we use. If we did, the judge would be throwing out cases left and right."

"He was very convincing, or at least he convinced me…a little. He did submit to the blood test after all."

Slim leans forward, as if he's about to tell me something that I shouldn't go repeating. "Listen, there's submitting to a drug test and volunteering for a drug test."

"What's the difference?"

"I believe you ACL types call it duress."

"ACLU—so then they forced him to take that drug test?"

"No…not exactly. He could've refused, but likely that would've put him in worse trouble than he's in now…and that point would've been made very clear to him. The reason I'm telling you this is because I want you to understand that just because somebody submits to a blood test doesn't mean they believe the test will come back negative; it just means that they're out of options and hoping to beat the test by—I don't know—

thinking positive thoughts...or I guess, negative thoughts in this instance."

"He seemed so sincere though about trying to get his life in order. He was a virtual font of self-help slogans and platitudes when I gave him a ride to where he's staying now."

"Those are just the types of things a guilty person would say."

"They're also the types of things an innocent person would say," I reply. "In case you didn't know it, they tend to say the same things."

"By the way, where is he staying? I know the Big Farm won't take him back because of their zero-tolerance policy."

"He's at...my place," I answer with embarrassment. "Doesn't it strike you as odd that he's passed so many drug tests on the Farm, but then he just happens to get into an accident that wasn't even his fault, and that's when he tests positive?"

"It doesn't strike me as odd at all. Usually, when the inmates get to leave the Farm, they're on the buddy system so they can keep an eye on each other, but from the report I read, Rod was sent on a last-minute errand alone. Probably the first time he'd been by himself in a vehicle in months. He saw his opportunity to get high and took it. If you want some free advice—"

"I don't," I say, sounding like Vance.

"Then if you want some friendly advice, I think you're too close to this thing. Let the process run its course. It's going to be whatever it's going to be...uh...irregardless of how you feel about it."

"The correct word you're fumbling for is either 'regardless' or 'irrespective.' "

"I don't care about the whichy-why of the correct word. I care about you and Becky and her kids."

I move the sugar pourer and the bowl of single-serve creamers out of the way of the napkin dispenser and extract a folded napkin to blow my nose.

"Why do you want to get mixed up in this thing anyway?" Slim asks in an easier tone. "What's Rod to you…besides a hassle that you don't need?"

"He's the father to a pair of boys that happen to be important to me."

"As far as I can tell, he ain't been much of a father to them boys."

"There's still a chance that he could be since they aren't grown yet, but if he goes to prison, they will be by the time he gets out." I dab under my nose. "I couldn't do anything for the McCormick boy, but maybe I can do something for these boys. I'm hollering for help here."

"All right then," Slim replies. "I got a plan."

Chapter 7

This town has about the same number of churches as bars and as many pawnshops as both of them put together…way more than you might think a community this size would require. Slim tells me we've only been to half of them so far, but I'm still not quite sure what it is that we're looking for. We exit Slim's squad car and walk toward the entrance of Peter's Three Sphere Pawn Emporium—sounds classy.

"Do you think this place sells Kleenex?" I ask.

"I've never heard of a pawnshop that does," Slim answers. "Can't imagine there's much of a market for secondhand tissue."

"I need to blow my nose again, but I'm out of napkins from the coffee shop."

"Then do a farmer blow."

"What's that?"

"You city boys." Slim shakes his head. "Press your finger against the side of your nose to close one nostril and then blow the snot out the other nostril onto the ground."

"But I've got snot in both nostrils."

"Then reverse and repeat the process," Slim says as if talking to a slow child.

I give it a try. The first attempt results in mucus running down my chin—disgusting. But I'm desperate here and not a quitter, so I try the other side. I put my back into the blow, and mucus shoots out of my nose at a surprising velocity, landing on Slim's boot. I can't remember the last time I felt so accomplished.

"Not bad." Slim balances on one foot and wipes the top of his boot against the back of his uniform's pant leg. "Good distance for a beginner."

We enter the pawnshop and fall into our now familiar routine. I sort of lurk in the background, browsing the shelves for I'm not really sure what— "something that looks out of place" Slim had said. The last pawnshop we visited had a complete set of encyclopedias—that seemed out of place among all the power tools and used electronics, but I didn't bring it to his attention. For his part, Slim talks to the proprietor, in this case, Pete, I assume. From what I've been able to overhear, Slim always keeps the interviews conversational…not like an interrogation that might provoke the shopkeeper to ask to see a warrant.

"The chief sent me over here to see if you've had any folks from the Big Farm come in lately. We're not lookin' for no stolen goods, so don't go thinking that I aim to relieve you of any of your inventory as evidence or nothing like that. He just wants me to find out if any of them Farm boys have been in here, trying to put a little money in their pockets. If you ask me, this is a waste of my time and yours, but then…you know, he's my boss, and he don't ask my opinion."

"I worked in the coal mines for twenty years before I finally saved enough to get out and open this here store, so I know how it is to work all damn day for some idiot above you. I did have a fella come in here yesterday about this time with a banjo. Gave me some song and dance about needing money to pay for his mama's funeral. He did mention in passing that he worked out at the Big Farm. It's a real nice banjo…I intend to put it on display in the front window, but truth be told, I lowballed him on my offer since I could tell he was desperate."

"Did this fella sell or pawn the banjo?"

"Pawned it, which is a bit peculiar these days…especially for somebody who looked to be hard up for money."

"Interesting," Slim says.

"If you think that's interesting, then what I tell you next will be downright thought-provoking. This fella said he'd be back in tomorrow about the same time with an accordion to pawn."

"This fella said that yesterday, meaning he'll be in again today…right about this time?"

"Any time now…if he keeps his word, which I expect he will as the desperate ones always show up when they tell you if they think there's money to be had."

Chapter 8

We wait inside Slim's squad car in the gravel parking lot outside the pawnshop for twenty minutes before I work up the courage to say, "I still don't get it."

"What don't you get?" Slim asks.

"This guy who happens to be an inmate at the Big Farm also happens to be hard up for money…so what?"

"Is that all we learned?"

"Yes."

"No."

"What else did we learn, oh wise one?"

"Have you ever played a banjo?" Slim asks.

"Answering a question with a question—how I enjoy that…no, I've never played a banjo, or a washboard, or a jug for that matter."

"Well, a banjo is mighty hard to play. Anybody can learn to strum a guitar and play a few chords, but learning to play the banjo takes years of practice…so long, in fact, that a fella would likely develop an attachment to his instrument."

"So you're saying that this guy wouldn't part with his banjo unless he absolutely had to."

"Bingo," Slim says as if I'd won something.

"But he told the pawnbroker that he needed the money for his mother's funeral—that seems like a pretty good reason."

"Nah, around here banjos get passed down through the family…sometimes for generations. No mother, living or dead, would be at peace with her son parting with his banjo on her account."

"He wasn't though…right?" I ask hesitantly. "The pawnbroker said he pawned it, and if I understand how pawnshops operate, that means he could get it back later."

"If he's desperate enough to part with his banjo, then he'd want as much money as he could get for it, which means he'd sell it rather than pawn it. When I saw this morning that you were the one who posted Rod's bail, it got me thinking about why he didn't pay his own bail. He's been out at that farm for a while now with nothing to spend his money on, so I reckoned that he must've had some cash saved. I asked around a bit, and found out—"

"—that they don't get paid until they complete their program, and they don't know for sure when that'll be, so…"

"So probably our guy doesn't know when he'd have the money to get his banjo out of hock…it could be months from now, by which point the term of the loan would've expired, and the pawnbroker will likely have sold it. Also, didn't you think it odd that he's coming back today with an accordion? Who plays the banjo and the accordion?"

"Then you think these aren't his instruments." I'm still trying to puzzle this all out. "You think he might be pawning things that belong to other inmates…maybe the missing inmates, and in case they do return soon, he could potentially reclaim their instruments. I imagine that the Farm doesn't exactly allow its inmates to bring all sorts of stuff with them, so these instruments must've been pretty dear, which begs the question: why did the inmates leave them behind when they left the Farm?"

"Bingo," Slim says again.

"I wish you'd stop with the 'bingos' already. So what do the missing inmates have to do with Rodney? He's not missing."

"Nope, we know right where his ass is...your place, doing who knows what. I don't claim to understand all the angles yet, but sometimes you gotta take a shot into a dark cave and then wait to see what runs out."

"Doesn't whatever's inside run out at you?"

"I said I had a plan; I never said—"

"I know," I interrupt, "you never said it was a good plan. But what if—"

"First rule of the stakeout: No 'what if' questions."

"Why not?"

"Second rule of the stakeout: No 'why not' questions."

"Is the third rule of the stakeout: No 'what do you think that guy has in the case' questions?"

"Nope, the third rule of the stakeout is no eating beans." Slim eyes the young man walking toward the pawnshop. "That's either an accordion he's got in there or the world's biggest typewriter."

"What do we do?" I ask. "Play good cop, bad cop?"

"We do nothing." Slim opens the driver's side door. "I play good cop, and you play pedestrian who happens to be walking by while keeping his mouth shut."

Slim gets out of the police cruiser, but before he can say anything, the young man spots the uniform, drops the accordion, and runs back to the cargo van he pulled up in. Slim gets back in the squad car just as I get out. Before I can reopen my door, Slim has started the car, put it into gear, and spun his tires, sending gravel spitting in my direction.

Slim races across the parking lot to where the van is parked and slams on the brakes just as the man rushes to get into the driver's seat. Slim puts the cruiser in park behind the van, blocking any chance of it being used as a getaway vehicle. He exits the squad car once again, while the young man looks around frantically as if deciding in which direction to run.

"You stay right there, dammit," Slim orders. "You ain't in no trouble yet, but if you make me chase your ass, you're gonna be in a whole heap of it."

The young man seems to consider his options. Then his expression transitions from fright to resignation. He extends his arms straight up as if a touchdown has been scored.

"Put your damn hands down." Slim approaches the young man. "Son, I already told you that you ain't in no trouble...I just want to talk with you for a minute."

I walk over with the case. "Hey, you dropped this."

"That's not mine," the young man says more to Slim than me.

"Son, I believe it ain't yours in that it don't belong to you, but I just saw you drop the damn thing right before you tried to run off."

I attempt to hand the young man the case, but he won't take it. Slim shakes his head at me, which I interpret to mean that I shouldn't give the probable perpetrator back the likely stolen item.

"Listen, I know this here accordion ain't yours," Slim says, "but what I don't know is how you got it, and I don't like not knowing things. Now you tell me what I don't know, and it'll help me make up my mind about what I'm going to do with you."

The young man eyes Slim warily. "I…I work out at the Big Farm."

"I know that too," says Slim. "Don't waste my time telling me things I already know. Tell me who it belongs to."

"I don't know," the young man says. "I swear."

"All right then," Slim replies. "Tell me how you got it."

"A team leader…a guard out at the Farm gives me things to sell sometimes. Then he sends me on an errand with the van so I can come into town…we split the money."

"Why doesn't he sell them himself?" Slim asks.

"Because they're not his."

"Then whose are they?" asks Slim.

"They belong to other inmates out at the Farm…the ones who've disappeared."

"Bingo," Slim says. "So the guard gives you these items, which they probably keep locked up out there, but the guard figures nobody will miss them because their owners have been gone for so long…then you sell them at a pawnshop for some quick cash. Son, you're taking all the risk in this little caper but only getting half the profit. That ain't too smart…especially if you're already on parole."

"I know, Officer, but I need the money."

"For what?" Slim asks. "Your mama's funeral…something like that?"

"No…I got a kid sister," the young man answers. "She needs braces real bad."

"Braces?" Slim looks heavenward with a goofy smile on his face. "Don't that beat all."

"She's twelve…going on thirteen. Her teeth are as crooked as a dog's hind legs, and you know how girls that age can be about their appearance. I've never been much of a role model to her. If you want to know the truth of it, I've been a pretty lousy brother, but braces are the only thing she's ever asked me for, so now I got a chance to do something for her, on account that our mom lost her job and can't afford them. I promise I'm not a bad guy…just made some bad choices is all. I don't even sell the stuff the guard gives me. I pawn it instead, just in case the inmates come back and whatever they left behind has sentimental value for them."

"Ain't that sweet," Slim says. "Okay, I got one last question. You answer it to my liking, and I'll cut you loose. If not, then you and me are taking a ride to the police station. What's this guard's name?"

"Jesse."

"Jesse what?"

"I don't know," the young man says. "They only use their first names out there…just like the guards in the prisons."

"Jesse ain't going to cut it," says Slim. "There are too many Jesses around for that to be of any use…maybe if you'd said Jehoshaphat that'd be different, but I can't track down every—"

"I hear him talking to the other guards sometimes about the Shady Tree. He likes to hang out at that tavern…a lot from what I gather."

Slim looks up again, as if mulling the situation over. Then he looks at me. "Civilian, on behalf of the local police department, I thank you for returning that there accordion, which rightly belongs to this gentleman."

I look at Slim and then the young man and then back at Slim, before I finally hand over the accordion case.

"Now listen good," Slim says to the young man who looks as confused as I feel, "you go pawn that accordion and then split the money with Jesse like you always do, and don't you tell him nothing about this conversation of ours…all he needs to know is that everything went smoothly."

"Oh…okay," the young man stammers.

"But the next time that guard suggests this little arrangement, you tell him no…flat out. You do your time and keep yourself to yourself. You understand me?"

"Yes, Officer."

With that Slim pulls out his wallet and hands the young man a hundred-dollar bill. "This here is to help with your sister's teeth."

The young man sheepishly accepts the bill. "Thank you, Officer."

Slim walks back to his squad car. I pull out my own wallet and hand the young man all the cash I have: two twenties and a five. I'm tempted to give him an unused gift card I've been carrying around for years to the City Winery, but then I figure it probably won't do his kid sister much good.

Chapter 9

Slim got in my head about Rodney staying at my place unsupervised. If he really is off the wagon and possibly feeling like I usurped his role in his family, then there's no telling what he might be up to, though several horrific scenarios play in my mind as I drive to my house. I can't help thinking of that story Becca told me about the hand grenade.

I park out front and am pleased to see that the house is not on fire and appears to be intact. I climb the front porch stairs with a bag of groceries and enter. I find Rodney asleep on my couch while some banal court show plays on the television—seems an odd choice. He wakes when I put the bag of groceries on the coffee table.

"Hey," Rodney says groggily, "I didn't hear you come in."

"No problem." I sit down in my recliner. "I brought you a few things. I know I told you to help yourself to whatever's in the freezer, but I thought you could use some fresh fruit...and there's bread and lunch meat in there too if you want to make some sandwiches."

"Thanks, man." He sits up and winces. "I don't know how to repay you."

"Don't worry about that now. Are you feeling okay?"

"I woke up this morning and my head hurt. My stomach has been doing somersaults ever since."

"Are you coming down with something?"

"Maybe…though it feels more like a really bad hangover," Rodney answers and then quickly adds, "but don't worry—I didn't touch your liquor cabinet."

I completely forgot about that. I suppose there's nothing that can be done about it now, though I do a quick mental inventory of anything else that I might've overlooked.

"Honestly," Rodney continues, "I've been asleep on the couch here for most of the day."

"That's a rough break…your first day of freedom and you spend it under the weather." I take several tissues from the Kleenex box on the coffee table and shove them into my coat pocket. "I can empathize…I've got a bit of a cold myself. Maybe a home-cooked meal would help. I'm headed over to Rebecca's place for dinner. You're welcome to come with me if you want. I know the boys would love to see you."

"I'd love to see them too, but I don't want them to see me run down like this, and I'd feel terrible if they caught whatever I have. Besides, I'm sure they'd have all sorts of questions, but everything is so up in the air until my hearing next week."

"Yeah, that makes sense." My tone is nonchalant, but I think I dodged a bullet there since the dinner offer just sort of popped into my head and then out of my mouth before I thought it through. I imagine Becca would've been a bit cross with me for bringing her ex-husband over unannounced—surprise. "So what are you hoping the outcome of your hearing will be?"

"I'm hoping that I don't have to go to prison, though that seems pretty unlikely considering the circumstances."

"What do you figure the best case scenario is?" I ask, though I'm not quite sure why.

"It'd be great if the Farm would see fit to give me a second chance. Maybe I could convince them to give me another drug test and show them...but that's a real long shot. They've got very strict rules about that sort of thing."

"Surely there are other programs. Given the time you've spent out at the Farm and the progress you've made, perhaps they'd just consider this a hiccup...a little blip on the radar." I become distracted by a vague notion in the back of my mind, losing my train of thought.

"I don't know...anything is better than prison, but starting over with another program doesn't sound so good either."

"Maybe you'd do even better in a different program...maybe finish sooner. Who knows, this could all turn out in your favor."

"You might be right," Rodney says without sounding like he really believes it. "But the Farm would be my first choice."

"What is it about the Farm that you're so partial to? It sounds like they work you hard, and you've been out there for quite a while, but it seems like your program might go on for some time still...not to mention the fact that you haven't been paid yet for all your efforts."

"Yeah," Rodney says, appearing confused. "When you put it like that, it doesn't sound like such a great deal…but there's just something about the Farm that I'd miss."

Chapter 10

I'm distracted during dinner with Becca and the boys. I keep mulling over what Rodney said about the Big Farm...not so much his words but more his sense of attachment to the place. I thought he would be glad to have a break from the work—whatever it is that they do out there during the winter, though as I've come to understand, farm work is never really done—but Rodney seemed truly lost, although I suppose having a prison sentence hanging over you could bring anyone down...or maybe he's been out there so long that he's become institutionalized. Still, something that I can't quite bring into focus seems wrong.

"What's wrong?" Becca asks.

"I honestly have no idea," I answer.

"Is it the corn?" she asks. "The boys like it when I mix it in with the mashed potatoes—pretty much the only way I can get them to eat canned corn when corn on the cob is out of season—but I understand if it's not your thing."

I look down at my plate and see kernels of corn in the mashed potatoes. I hadn't noticed them when I scooped the potatoes onto my plate.

"That's very inventive," I say. "I liked to mix corn into my mashed potatoes when I was a kid too."

"Our dad used to tell us that they were made from special potatoes," Lance says. "Corn-taters he called them. He said they grew above ground on stalks, but it was a lie…just like Santa Claus."

"It's tough, isn't it?" I ask Lance.

"What?"

"Discovering just how many lies our generation has told yours…the Easter Bunny, the Tooth Fairy, the possibility of retirement."

"Tell me about it." He drinks his milk the way a wino drinks Night Train.

"One of my clients mentioned that she saw you coming out of a pawnshop earlier today," Becca informs me.

"Yeah, Slim took me to a few," I reply. "Tonight we're going to someplace called the Shady Tree."

"He's really gone out of his way to show you the nicer parts of town," Becca says.

"You're going to the Shady Tree?" Vance asks, apparently impressed.

"How do you know about the Shady Tree?" asks Becca.

"I am in high school, Mom…people talk."

"What do they say when they talk about the Shady Tree?" I ask.

"They say don't go there," Van tells me.

"I'm with Vancy on this one," Becca adds. "That place is bad news."

Chapter 11

Slim pulls his truck into Becca's driveway. I bid the boys a good night and give Becca a kiss. I stuff my parka pockets full of Kleenex before I leave.

I get into the cab of the truck. "Becca seems to think this Shady Tree place might be a little rough."

"Might be." Slim backs out of the drive.

"Yeah, but don't you know all the bars in town?"

"I know of it."

"You mean all the time you've spent drinking at bars around here, and you've never been to this one?"

"Well, it ain't exactly my crowd."

"What type of crowd is it?" I ask.

"Mostly prison and security guards."

"That sounds like your kind of people to me."

"It's the same church but different pew," Slim clarifies. "The bar is a hangout for the Ebony Enforcers—a black motorcycle gang...and don't give me that liberal look of yours. It ain't segregation if both sides agree to it. We just got different taste in music is all."

"But you said they're all prison and security guards, so you have a sort of fraternal kinship with them, right?"

"I said they're mostly prison and security guards, which ain't exactly the same thing as being police...or at least not everybody sees it that way. Don't get me wrong, they ain't outlaw types. The majority of them are good old boys who just happen to prefer a jukebox stocked with rhythm and blues to one with country and western, but it's still a biker gang. We can't expect to go up in there, pretty as you please, asking a bunch of questions about one of their members."

"So what are we going to do then?"

"We're going to go there, order a couple of drinks, check the place out, and see what we can see."

"The old shot-in-the-dark technique."

"Yeah, but keep that talk about shooting at things that are dark to yourself when we get there."

"You know that's not remotely what I meant."

"Your prejudices are your affair." Slim smiles that smile he gets when he thinks he's being clever. "It's a free country. You can speak your mind how you want, just so long as you don't go breaking the law."

"I'm not the benighted rube who talks like he has a third-grade education."

"I see how you are…you derogate the underprivileged and the undereducated alike," Slim says with that same stupid smile. "If you ain't the be-all and end-all of the ivory tower set."

"That phrase 'be-all and end-all' comes from Macbeth. I bet you didn't know that you were quoting Shakespeare just now…dummy."

Chapter 12

Slim and I look out of place when we walk into the Shady Tree, him wearing a Carhartt coat and me a Gore-Tex parka in a barroom full of so many leather jackets…and also we're the only white guys in sight.

Per our stupid plan, we split up so as to attract less attention, which is absolutely impossible. As I make my way to the bar, I feel as if I stand out like an errant stalk of wheat growing in a field of soybeans. Great, now I'm thinking in similes that make me sound like a hayseed. At the bar, I order a Scotch on the rocks. The bartender stares at me sideways and gives me an are-you-sure-you're-in-the-right-place sort of look. Then he informs me that as close as he can get is Crown Royal. Fine, I tell him, at least it's an imported whisky.

I drink my Canadian whisky and look around the barroom, trying to seem as inconspicuous as the circumstances will allow. I notice the insignia of the Ebony Enforcers on several jackets—a riff on the Jolly Roger: a black skull with two crossed nightsticks below it…cuddly stuff. I swivel back around on my barstool and inadvertently make eye contact with a big guy three stools down.

"It's getting awful bright in here," the large man says…to me, I guess. "Did somebody turn up the lights?"

I look around, but nobody seems to be paying the big fella any attention, aside from me, and I'm trying not to.

"I said it's getting bright in here," the man states more stridently. "Did the sun come up early?"

"Cool it, James." An attractive gal with an afro walks over from a nearby table. "He's with me."

"I don't like it," the man informs us.

"And I don't like that your head is so fat," the woman replies.

I laugh a little, but then the bruiser growls, so I keep quiet and follow the lady's lead back to her table.

"Thanks for the save," I say as I sit down. "Do I know you?"

"Nope, but I know you Weston Payley. I heard that you'd moved to town awhile back, and I recognize you from your picture on the book jacket of *Swahili Spinster*…though just barely. You look different than I thought you would."

"If I recall correctly, the photographer for that one was going for dark and mysterious."

"No, I mean you look older."

"Yes, well, I did write that book some years ago."

"So what are you doing here now?" She stirs the ice in her highball glass. "Research?"

"Of a sort…I've been looking into the Big Farm, and as I understand it, some of the prison guards—or team leaders as I believe they're called—frequent this establishment."

"Yeah, I think some of the guards do come here from time to time. What is it that you want to know?"

"It's kind of a I-don't-know-what-I-don't-know situation." I sip my whisky. "I just have a hunch."

"Sounds intriguing."

"Maybe, though judging from all the stares that I'm getting, I doubt if I'll find anyone too cooperative."

"Let them stare…it's not every day that we get a celebrity in here."

"The guy near the jukebox has been giving me the side-eye pretty hard since we sat down, and I don't think he's working up the courage to ask for an autograph. He's not your boyfriend or something like that, is he?"

"Absolutely not," she says with a charming laugh. "I wouldn't date anyone who comes here."

Before I can respond with anything charming of my own, someone forcefully bumps into the back of my chair. I turn to see Slim standing over me.

"Time to go, partner."

"I was just having a lovely conversation with…" I say, turning my attention back to my table companion. "I'm sorry, I didn't catch your—"

"You can catch her name later," Slim interrupts. "We've got to go now."

I look past Slim to see several large men approaching. The leader is brandishing a pool cue menacingly.

"This all feels rather familiar." I quickly rise to leave.

"You can tell me about it in the comfort of my Cadillac." Slim hustles me toward the exit.

"Nice meeting you," I call over my shoulder.

Once we hit the door, Slim makes a hard left, pulling me along with him. We duck behind the corner of the building as the group of men following us emerges from the bar. They fan out and search the parking lot, looking in the windows of Eldorados and Escalades. Soon the men get cold and head back inside.

I let out a sneeze I'd been stifling. "That was pretty smart letting everyone think you drive a Cadillac."

"This ain't my first rodeo."

We start walking toward his truck.

"Really…you've done this before?"

"This here? Nah, this is the first time I've ever attempted such foolishness."

Chapter 13

Slim pulls out of the parking lot, keeping his headlights off until we cross the road. Then we pull into a used car lot that offers a view of the tavern. He parks his pickup between two other trucks and kills the engine.

"So what was that all about?" I ask.

"I guess they got different rules for shooting pool around here," he answers.

"Our objective wasn't to win a pool game."

"Nope, our objective was to agitate and see what shakes loose. Hand me them field glasses inside the glove box."

"You've got a real knack for the agitating part— I'll give you that." I open the glove compartment and pass Slim the binoculars located within. We watch the front door of the bar for a few minutes. I think I recognize the first person we see exit. "Can I have a look at those?" Slim hands me the binoculars, and I'm able to confirm that it's the guy who'd been standing near the jukebox. "That's the guy who was fish-eyeing me."

"Are you kidding? All I got in there were sideways eyeballs."

"But he was fish-eyeing me so hard that I wouldn't be surprised if he knew how to breathe underwater."

"You think he recognized you…like maybe from your visit to the Big Farm?"

"Maybe…he looks vaguely familiar, but I'm not a hundred percent sure."

"Why?" Slim asks with his trademark smile of stupidity. "Because you think people with a dark complexion all look the same?"

"No, of course not. It was months ago when I was out there. Are we really back on this again?"

"You're the one who brought it up by saying they all look alike…you have to learn to see past skin color."

"Are you quite finished? So are we going to follow this guy or what?"

"There ain't no 'or what' about it." Slim fires up his truck and revs the engine just as the man pulls out of the parking lot in a late-model Corvette. Slim trails him without following too closely, but the car begins to increase speed as it heads toward the main road. "I don't know if he realizes that we're tailing him, or if he's just a guy who likes to drive fast."

"Do you want me to take down his license plate number?"

"Can you read it from here?"

"No," I admit.

"Then why'd you ask?"

"Maybe with the binoculars—"

"You can try, though this backroad is a might bumpy, and this old Ford is many things but smooth ain't one of them."

I put the binoculars up to my eyes, but I'm being jostled too much to train them on the car's plate. "I can't tell if it starts with an 'A' or a 'Z' or one of the letters in between."

"All right then—hang on." Slim hammers down on the accelerator and flips an aftermarket toggle switch on the dashboard. Suddenly I see blue and red lights flashing from the front of the truck. Slim must have police lights installed in the grill. "My pickup has plenty of pickup, and I ain't no slouch of a driver, but if this dude decides to rabbit on us, once he hits that main road, there ain't much chance of us catching him."

The Corvette slows down slightly, as if the driver is trying to make up his mind. Then in a burst of violent acceleration, the sports car quickly begins to pull away.

"Shoot," says Slim. "I was fifty-fifty on whether I should hit the red and blues…now he knows we were tailing him."

It doesn't take long for the Corvette to get far ahead of us, but just before the car reaches the intersection, it spins out—its headlights momentarily facing toward us—and slams sideways into a ditch. It takes us several seconds to catch up to it, Slim being cautious not to skid on the same patch of ice.

Slim parks his truck on the side of the road above the crashed car. We both get out to examine the vehicle. The damage is extensive. The Corvette's big rear end, housing four circular taillights, is no longer attached to the car. The driver's side door is open. Judging from the driver's bloodied face, the now deflated airbag must've hit him hard, but he's conscious, though still stunned.

"Do you need medical attention?" Slim calls down to him.

The man glances from side to side and then up at us. He looks at Slim as if confused, but then he spots me, and his expression becomes that of concern. "I'm…I'll be okay."

173

"Your name wouldn't happen to be Jesse, would it?" Slim asks. "Jesse who works as a guard out at the Big Farm?"

The man looks down but doesn't respond. Slim carefully descends into the ditch and hands him a handkerchief. "Here, press this against that gash on your forehead."

Jesse takes the handkerchief and does as he's instructed. I climb down the embankment and take position next to Slim.

"Now see here," Slim says, "I got you for evading and reckless driving, and I bet I could think of some other stuff too, which I doubt would do much for your career...or depending on how cooperative you're willing to be, we could just call your busted rocket ship punishment enough for all that."

Jesse looks at Slim as he dabs his forehead and holds his neck. Then he looks over at me. "I don't know...what is it that you want?"

"Just answers to a few questions is all," Slim replies. "For starters, how is it that you know my partner?"

"I don't know him...I know of him," Jesse answers. "After he came out to the Farm last summer, Dr. Jude put a picture of him up in the staff room—told us to let him know if he came sniffing around again."

"Well, he is nosy," Slim says, "but why were you so bothered when you saw him tonight? Does it have something to do with a certain errand you sent an inmate on today?"

"I thought you might know about that," Jesse replies as he looks at me. "Seemed like quite a coincidence that I'd send one of my guys to fetch a hush-hush shipment from the airport, and then he shows up a few hours later."

"Hold on…fetch?" I blurt. "I thought you sent him to sell an accordion?"

"Let the man finish his story," Slim tells me.

"Accordion…no, I figured you wanted to know about the shipment?"

"We want to know about both," Slim clarifies. "What did your man pick up at the airport?"

"I don't know…and that's what was strange about it," Jesse answers. "Usually we get a manifest so our guys know what they're picking up, but I was told yesterday to send just one inmate for today's shipment…a young guy who won't ask questions to retrieve something from a private plane, but when he got back to the Farm, he was all jittery, even though he said everything went smoothly."

"That does sound strange," Slim says. "So what was in the shipment?"

"Hey, man, you're asking questions above my pay grade," Jesse answers. "They only tell us enough to give orders to the prisoners…I mean patients."

"Come on, Jesse," Slim says with frustration. "Take a guess…was the shipment small, like a package of pills, or bigger than a breadbox?"

"Pills?" asks Jesse. "No, it was a big crate with four unmarked canisters inside…each about the size of an oil drum. We started to uncrate it when the driver got back to the Farm like we usually do, but then Dr. Jude came out to the machine shed and told us he'd do it himself later, which was also strange."

"The professor doing manual labor...that would qualify as strange," I reply. "So then what's the deal with the accordion?"

"That?" Jesse asks. "Every once in a while I give one of my guys something to sell at a pawnshop for some extra cash that we split...just old junk from the storage lockup that nobody will miss."

"How do you know they won't miss it?" I ask.

"What do you mean?" asks Jesse. "It's just stuff left behind by the inmates who've gone missing."

"What he means is how do you know that the inmates won't be coming back for it?" Slim asks pointedly.

Jesse looks down again. "Man, listen...I don't know the half of what goes on at the Big Farm, and I don't want to know. You need to talk somebody higher up the food chain if you want answers to the kinds of questions you're asking, but that shipment today ain't the only strange shit that's ever happened out there."

"I like strange stories," Slim says, "so tell us another one."

"About eight months ago, I was given a detail of men to take out into this field that was lying fallow and dig a hole near an old oak tree...a big hole. Whatever, I figured work was slow, so they were trying to give the inmates something to do...keep 'em busy. I thought in a few days they'd send me back out with different guys to fill the hole back in."

"But they never did?" asks Slim.

"Nope," Jesse answers, "and as far as I know, they didn't send anybody else out there either, but a few weeks later, I was in that same field, and—"

"The hole was filled in," I say.

"Yep," Jesse replies. "Like I said…strange shit."

"All right then, Jesse," Slim says, "I ain't telling you this is over, but your part is done for now. Do you want a lift back to the bar?"

"I can manage on my own," Jesse answers. "No offense, but I don't think it's a good idea for me to be seen with you guys."

"I read you," Slim says, "but this thing cuts both ways, so I need you to read me. Nobody was chasing you tonight…you were driving home—maybe a little too fast—and a deer ran out in front of you, so you swerved to miss it, crashing your race car."

"I read you loud and clear."

Chapter 14

It's been ages since I've been back on campus. The quad looks the same, but everything around it has changed. The surrounding blocks that were once home to crappy coffee shops and terrible taverns have been replaced by cafés with familiar logos and chain restaurants that all look like they're owned by the same tchotchke-obsessed corporation. I suppose this is progress, though of the insipid variety.

I walk the snowy sidewalks, searching for the last address Edwin gave me. He usually hibernates in winter since the heating system out at the radio telescope was only designed to keep the instruments from freezing. I would've called first, but despite being a man of science, Edwin is very much a Luddite and believes the expense of a cell phone to be frivolous. He usually gets a little down during the wintertime, so I thought I'd try to raise his spirits by taking him out for lunch and maybe pick his brain about things that come in canisters.

I find Ed's building, but on the way over, I'd inadvertently smudged the apartment number on the slip of paper with his address when, during a mucus emergency, I absentmindedly used it to wipe my nose. I look up at the balconies on the side of the building. All but one contain snow-covered grills and bicycles—top floor, far corner.

I climb the stairs and knock on the door. An attractive, middle-aged woman wearing a man's bathrobe answers the door. I'm caught off guard and unable to find any suitable words. Not only is she not who I was expecting to open the door, but the tattered robe notwithstanding, I wouldn't have thought a woman of her apparent class would reside in an apartment building full of rowdy college students.

"I don't want to tell you how to do your job," she says, "but I believe it's customary for the pizza delivery man to actually bring the pizza with him when he knocks on the door."

"Does Edwin live here?" I ask tentatively.

"Yes, but I'm the one who placed the order."

"No, I'm not a delivery guy. I'm Weston...Ed's friend."

"Oh, I'm terribly sorry," she says. "Yes, Eddie is taking a shower, but he'll be out in a few moments. You can come inside and wait for him if you like."

"I don't want to be a bother...perhaps I should come back later."

"It's no bother." She steps out of the doorway and beckons me in. "I haven't met any of Eddie's friends yet, but he's mentioned you on several occasions. We were just about to have some lunch...you're welcome to join us."

"Thanks." I enter the small, spartanly furnished apartment. "A slice of pizza does sound tempting."

"So you're the writer." She takes a seat on a folding chair. "My name is Kate, by the way."

"It's a pleasure to meet you." I consider sitting on a beanbag chair and then think better of it. I can hardly believe Ed still has that thing, though I suppose as furniture goes, beanbag chairs are easy to pack up and move. "Have you known, uh…Eddie a long time?"

"Off and on for a few years…you know."

"Apparently I don't."

Edwin emerges from the steamy bathroom with a towel wrapped around his waist. Robes seem to be at a premium in this apartment. He looks as surprised to see me standing in his living/dining room as I was to see Kate standing in his doorway.

"Weston!"

"Well, I'll let you two get caught up while I go change." Kate rises and walks toward the bedroom. "The pizza will be here soon, Eddie."

"Eddie?" I ask after Kate closes the bedroom door. "I thought you hated that name."

"I don't mind it the way she says it."

"So why haven't you told me about her before?"

"We've been off and on for a few years now."

"So I've heard."

"I'm just not sure what sort of future we'd have. You know how I am when it comes to understanding humans…the brainy imbecile who typically has no idea what people are talking about when they invoke the phrase 'for obvious reasons.' "

"She seems nice…maybe go with your feelings and let the future worry about itself."

"I think that makes more sense for you than it does for me," replies Ed. "Kate is one of a kind though. She's a behavioral neuroscientist, currently doing a fellowship here."

"It appears that's not the only fellow she's doing."

"Yes, very sophomoric…welcome back to campus. Speaking of being on campus, I showed Vance

Delacroix's transcript to a friend of mine, and she said if he raises his GPA and joins 4-H, she can get him admitted to the School of Agriculture, and then from there he can transfer into the School of Engineering after his freshman year, provided he gets good enough grades."

"Thanks, Ed, I owe you one."

"Forget it…maybe someday the kid will name a bridge after me. I've always wanted my own bridge."

"What have I told you about buying bridges?" Kate emerges from the bedroom in an evening gown. "You have to get a notarized contract…no handshake deals."

"Wow," I remark. "You really get dressed up to eat pizza."

"This old thing," Kate says as she strikes a pose. "My department had a black-tie fundraiser last night that I dragged Eddie to because I know how much he loves those sorts of events."

"Yes, luckily all the awkward small talk distracted me from how uncomfortable I felt in that ill-fitting rental tuxedo."

"Speaking of wearing clothes," Kate says, "perhaps you should go dress for lunch too."

I can't help but let out a chuckle. Kate and Ed both look at me with the same quizzical expression. "Sorry, it's just that Ed used that same phrase 'speaking of' a moment ago when you were in the other room."

"It's a common phrase," Ed replies. "I hear people use it all the time. It's not like we, you know…"

"Finish each other's sentences," Kate says with a grin.

"Right." Ed toddles off to the bedroom, seemingly unaware of the fun being had at his expense.

"So Ed mentioned that you're a neuroscientist."

"That's just a hobby really," says Kate. "My true calling is Kabuki acting."

"I'd think you were joking, but you do seem to have a bit of the performer in you."

"My apologies, I sometimes get carried away."

"Not at all," I reply. "Your personality is delightful…it's just that—if you don't mind my saying after only knowing you for a few minutes—you and Ed are so different and yet in some ways so similar."

"Eddie and I are poles apart, but we have a lot of overlap too, such as chemistry for instance."

"Sure, chemistry is important."

"No, I mean, I recently analyzed that sample you brought him last year and found it rather intriguing."

"How so?" I ask.

"The structures of some of the phytochemicals' constituents were similar to a few experimental synthetic opioids I've studied before, but Eddie said you got the sample from a drug rehab facility."

"Right, I see what you mean by intriguing. Could it get the patients high?"

"I doubt it, but it might partially mimic that particular pathophysiological state and suppress the cravings of a drug addict…like artificial sweetener can for someone who craves sugar."

"So it's harmless then?" I ask.

"Not necessarily. Take saccharin for example, which—fun fact—is a derivative of tar. It can quell cravings for sweetness by tricking the body into thinking that it has ingested sugar, but when the body gets confused like that, it can respond in physiologically deleterious ways that could result in metabolic derangement."

"Then you're saying this stuff could mess up someone's metabolism?"

"No," Kate answers with a frown that I've seen many times from Ed. "I was merely using saccharin as an analogy. I'm sure you're familiar with the concept...you being an author and all. I have no idea how those particular phytochemicals would affect somebody's brain chemistry—especially that of an addict whose opioid receptors may already be compromised. Making that determination would require a massive amount of research, long-term studies, and clinical trials."

"So then could this facility be engaging in some sort of Tuskegee experiment type scenario?"

"It's not impossible," Kate replies with a different sort of frown. "As you suggest, such a situation isn't without precedent, but that's the catch-22 of it all...you'd have to convince an entity with the resources to do the research that these drugs are harmful; however, from what Eddie mentioned, based on the treatment facility's success rate, the outcomes appear to fall in a range from benign to beneficial."

"Except a boy died."

"Yes, most unfortunate," Kate says with her most sorrowful frown yet. "I know I'm getting all this secondhand at best, but wasn't a toxicology examination conducted postmortem that found opioids in the boy's system?"

"That's correct," I answer, "but couldn't these phytochemicals have fooled the test...caused a false-positive?"

"Again, it's not impossible, but as I said, only some of the structures were similar to a few synthetic opioids I've seen before…not the same, and I wouldn't even have made that connection, if I hadn't happened to have been privy to a small study done a number of years ago. Before committing resources, a research organization would employ the old Occam's razor bit…is the simplest solution that this addict had a relapse and overdosed or that there's a massive conspiracy underway involving an eminent professor and a renowned addiction-recovery center. That weighed against all the unregulated, possibly pernicious nutritional supplements that are already on the market, I'm afraid the calculus is pretty cut and dry…and it doesn't favor your cause, but you're a crusader, so top marks for that."

"Okay," I say, taking a breath. "What do you know about canisters?"

"Canisters?" Ed asks, returning from the bedroom in jeans and a sweatshirt. "As I understand it, they're useful for storing things."

Chapter 15

Becca has her head in the freezer again, which I guess beats sticking it in the oven, though with her crazy pregnancy cravings lately, I suspect she's considered it.

"What about a frozen lasagna?" she asks.

"I think it sounds good," I answer, "but it won't be ready until about an hour after the boys' bedtime."

"Right...we could order a pizza."

"We just ordered pizza the other night." I decide not to mention that I also had pizza for lunch.

"Oh yeah...I forgot—pregnancy brain."

"If you're craving Italian again, I could whip up my famous spaghetti and meatballs."

"You know a good recipe?" she asks skeptically.

"I don't need a good recipe—just good ingredients: one box of pasta, one jar of sauce, one bag of frozen meatballs."

"That would be great, but we're out of marinara sauce."

"Do you have any ketchup and maybe a little oregano? The boys will never know the difference."

"I'll know the difference, and that sounds disgusting."

"What sounds disgusting?" Vance enters from the living room. "And what's for dinner? Is Moms still on her Italian kick?"

"That's a lot of questions, young man," I say. "Now I have one for you. How does joining 4-H sound?"

"I think it sounds mad stupid…doesn't 4-H stand for Hayseeds, Hicks, Hillbillies, and Clodhoppers?"

Not the enthusiasm I was hoping for. "That last one doesn't even start with an 'H.' "

"It's not like those illiterate dummies would know that," Van replies.

"You're one to talk about academics," I say, "which is why you need to join 4-H if you want to go to the university. I spoke to a friend of mine, and he can get you into the School of Ag if you raise your grades and have 4-H on your college application."

"Ag!" Van protests. "I don't want to be a farmer; I want to be a civil engineer."

"I know, but this is a way to do that," I reply. "Once you're in, you can transfer to the School of Engineering, if you keep your grade point average up."

"Why does everything have to be about numbers?"

"You mean unlike engineering?" I ask. "By the way, 4-H's slogan is 'learn by doing'…not learn by bitching."

"So?"

"You've got a real chance here to pursue your ambition," I say.

"So?"

"So take it," I answer, "and stop saying 'so.' "

"Or what…you'll quote the 4-H motto again?"

"I told you their slogan. The 4-H motto is 'To make the best better.' And to be your best self, you need to be better."

"Whatevs."

"Your language skills have really come a long way," I reply. "Perhaps one day soon you'll be ready to speak English."

With that Vance turns on his heels and exits the kitchen as if a teargas grenade had been detonated.

"That did not go the way I hoped it would," I inform Becca as if she hadn't just heard the whole exchange. "I pull some strings for the kid, and I get 'whatevs' as thanks."

"Let him process it," she says. "He'll come around. He's probably embarrassed that he needs help in the first place and scared that he might mess up a chance that he never thought he'd get." Becca kisses me, and I put my arms around her, which is no mean feat considering her circumference of late. Standing here in this kitchen is maybe the most at home I've ever felt. "Thanks for trying to help my son…you've been good to this family."

"I care about your boys…I know how it is to grow up with a father who's hardly ever around. For their sake, I wish I could do more to help Rodney. I checked on him again this afternoon, and he looks worse than he did yesterday."

"Take it from a social worker, you can only help the ones who want help."

Chapter 16

The headlights from Slim's truck shine through Becca's living room window, and I slide my stack of Monopoly money across the coffee table to Lance, which isn't very tall since I just had to pay through the nose to stay at Van's hotel on Boardwalk.

"What are you two up to tonight?" Becca asks.

"We're going to search for some unmarked graves."

"Don't make up stories like that in front of the boys," she admonishes. "They might not know that you're joking."

"Okay." I kiss her forehead. "I hate to leave in the middle of the game, especially since I was poised to make a comeback, but I'll see you boys in the morning."

"Good night, Won-Set," Lance says as I tousle his hair.

"So you've moved on to anagrams?"

"Yeah, since you were talking crazy about your chances of still winning this game, I thought I'd try to find a victory in your name…it's the best I could come up with on short notice."

"A winner in name only—I'll take it," I say. "Van, before I go, I want to ask if you still remember the 4-H slogan."

"Learn by mooing."

"Close enough for tonight." I put on my parka and check the pockets for Kleenex.

"Be safe, hon," Becca says.

I take one last look at them before I close the door. I must be dense to leave this warm home to go out into the cold, looking for who knows what.

As I open the passenger's side door of Slim's truck, I glance at the bed of the pickup. It's empty.

"You don't look so hot." Slim pulls out of the driveway.

"I can't shake this cold, and I just ate a microwaved lasagna that wasn't meant to be microwaved."

"Nothing like a home-cooked meal."

"Right—with Becca being in what seems like her fourth trimester, grocery shopping has fallen by the wayside."

"You two decided on a name for the little girl yet?"

"Becca wants to name the baby after her grandmother, and I want to name her Fellas-stay-away-or-my-father-will-kill-you."

"That don't exactly roll off the tongue."

"I could be talked into a shorter version, so long as Becca agrees that our daughter won't be allowed to date until she's thirty."

"My friend, I don't think fatherhood is going to go easy for you."

"Maybe not." I look out the back window. "So I thought you'd be bringing along a cadaver dog."

"Dogs are noisy, and we want to do this thing real quiet like, so we'll use a methane detector." Slim holds up a handheld device. "It ain't my cell phone."

"For a country cop, you've got a lot of high-tech toys."

Chapter 17

Slim deftly navigates the backroads and country lanes to the Big Farm. He's careful to avoid driving past the main complex so as not to arouse suspicion. The night is moonless, making it eerily dark. A fogbank hangs low over the fields we pass.

"I'm not seeing any oak trees," I remark.

"I'm not sure we'd see them in this fog even if they were there, but I know there's a big oak at the crossroads up ahead."

"We're out in the middle of nowhere. How do you know there's an oak tree ahead?"

"I've lived here all my life, so I know these roads pretty good. The tree we're coming up on is kind of a landmark. Back before the Big Farm, when these fields were part of regular little farms, me and my high school buddies would meet up at that oak after football games to drink beer."

"Sounds like a hoot and a half."

Slim pulls off to the side of the road. Near the desolate intersection ahead stands a gnarled, ancient oak; its bare limbs look like the outstretched fingers of a giant reaching up from his grave. I'm sure at some point in history a bluesman must've sold his soul to the devil here.

"This seems like a good place to bury a body," I say.

"Yeah, that old tree looked a lot less creepy when it was surrounded by teenagers drinking Budweiser."

We get out of the truck. The sound of us shutting the doors seems like it could travel for miles across these cold, empty fields. Slim starts pacing back and forth near the oak tree with the methane detector. I walk out into the field a ways. Decaying plant matter that's well on its way to breaking down into soil pokes through the patina of snow that covers the field. Off in the distance, a light twinkles through the fog and then vanishes. My granddad used to tell a story about the ghost of a bride who died in a carriage crash on the way to her wedding. Her ghost is said to roam these lonely country roads at night with a lantern, trying to find her way to the wedding she never had.

"I think I've got something here," Slim says. I walk back toward his location near the tree. He has one knee on the ground with the methane detector in hand. "I'm getting a strong read in this area." He uses his free hand to push away the snow cover, revealing a patch of bare soil. "And see how the dirt around here isn't covered by old cornstalks."

"Like it's been dug up."

"Yep, somebody's been digging out here."

"So should we get some shovels then?" I ask.

"Nah, the ground's frozen. It'd take heavy machinery to dig more than a foot or two."

"Do you really think we're standing on a mass grave for the missing inmates?"

"I don't know," Slim answers. "It could be buried coyotes that've been shot by a local farmer or the grave of a dog that got run over, but something's down there giving off methane, and I'd give my left nut to know what."

"Well, hopefully it won't come to that."

As Slim stands up, something in the old oak catches his attention. For a long moment, he studies a shadow where two tree branches meet, and then suddenly he turns to scan our surroundings.

"Shit—we need to go!" He begins to walk briskly back toward his truck.

"What is it?"

"There's a camera mounted up in that tree," Slim answers, "and it ain't there to watch over no canine's grave."

As I jog to catch up with Slim, I see the same twinkling light again in the foggy field...and then three more. I haven't any idea what's about to happen, but I know that it won't be good. I look back to the truck and see a cargo van quickly approaching. The van's headlights come on just as it skids to a stop on the gravel road, nearly slamming into the tailgate of the pickup. Slim bolts for the passenger's side door of his truck, but before he can open it, two men wearing ski masks and holding shotguns exit the van. They appear intent on not allowing Slim access to his vehicle.

I turn toward the field, thinking that I might have a chance to escape into the fogbank and make my way to the nearest farmhouse to phone for help. It seems I'm not the only one who considered that possibility. Four ATVs emerge from the fog, their headlights bouncing up and down over the uneven terrain of the field. As the ski-masked riders draw near, I see that each of them is either brandishing a pistol or has a rifle strapped across his back. I move toward Slim as the ATVs close in.

Slim backs in my direction as the two men with shotguns advance on him.

"Is your gun in the truck?" I whisper as we both put our hands up.

"I keep a snub-nosed revolver stuffed down in my bootleg. What do you think the odds are of me shooting all six of these dudes before one of them gets a shot off?"

"Slim to none."

"Cute," Slim replies.

"So what were you going for in your truck?"

"My two-way radio's under the seat. These boys got the drop on us real good. Our only chance out of this thing was to call in the cavalry."

"That wasn't too smart to leave it in the truck then."

"About as smart as having a cell phone in your pocket and not using it to call 911, opting instead to run all around like a chicken with its dang head cut off."

"Dammit," I say louder than a whisper. "I always forget I have that thing on me."

"Don't sweat it. You probably wouldn't have gotten reception out here anyways."

"That's enough chitchat out of you two," says one of the shotgunners.

"Dead or alive, you're going in the back of that van," the other says. He uses the shotgun he's holding to motion toward the van.

"Oh, that van over there," I say. "I wasn't sure which van you meant until you pointed to it with your gun."

"Weston, I've got to be honest with you," Slim says. "There's a little bit of me that hopes they shoot your ass."

Chapter 18

Slim and I are in the back of the windowless van, riding over rough roads at what feels like highway speeds. Our hands are zip-tied behind us. I've been relieved of my cell phone and Slim of his revolver. The masked gunman in the passenger's seat keeps his shotgun trained on us.

"That's a nice pump-action you've got there," I say. "I suppose if you're in the business of intimidation, you can't go wrong with that distinctive pumping sound. I only shoot break-action double-barrels myself. When it comes to a double-barrel, what do you prefer Slim…an over-and-under or a side-by-side?"

"We still talking about shotguns?"

"Shut your mouths," the gunman orders, "or I'll duct tape them shut."

"My bad," I reply. "I tend to prattle on when I get nervous, but I can't breathe through my nose just now, so I'll keep quiet…not another word."

The van slows and makes a sharp turn. The tires lose traction and slide. Beneath the van, we hear a cracking noise, putting me in mind of my fall through the ice earlier in the week. The van suddenly drops several inches with a loud splash, but after some spinning, the van's tires regain purchase and slosh through the water onto terra firma once more.

Soon the ride becomes smoother, and the van drives onward at a slower pace. After a short time, we come to a stop. The driver gets out and comes around to the back of the van, opening the rear doors, while the masked man sitting shotgun keeps an eye on us. Slim and I are pulled out of the van and marched from the edge of a field into a wooded area.

"I know these woods," Slim whispers. "This is where the entrance to that underground shooting range is located."

I look over my shoulder and confirm that the skeet shooting track is behind us. We're pushed along into the woods until the lead gunman instructs us to stop. Then he stoops to lift a camouflage netting covering what looks like a large cellar door. He unlocks the padlock and swings opens the heavy-duty metal door.

The lead gunman descends the subterranean stairs, and we are told to follow. I start to object, but the rear gunman sticks the muzzle of his shotgun into the small of my back, and I think better of it. The cinderblock corridor we enter seems little more than a tornado shelter, but as we walk farther down the passageway, I see an opaque glass door up ahead that looks out of place. The lead gunman opens the door and tells us to enter the large, partially lit room.

"Ah, our intrepid guests have arrived," says Dr. Weize. "What strange bedfellows the pair of you make."

"Mister, I think you done got the wrong idea about the nature of this here partnership," Slim replies.

"Strange indeed." Weize shakes his head at the rangemaster, who's standing nearby with an imposing handgun at the ready. "I must say, Mr. Payley, that you don't seem particularly surprised to see me."

"I knew you were at the center of this thing somehow," I reply.

"Hardly at the center. I am but the humble facilitator of an exceptional undertaking."

"We saw what kind of undertaker you are at that mass grave tonight," Slim responds.

"Thank you, gentlemen, for your assistance," Dr. Weize says to the two masked gunmen. "Would you be so good as to stand sentry out in the hallway and to close the door behind you? I think the rangemaster here can provide quite enough protection from these two."

The gunmen leave, pulling the substantial door shut as they exit the room. The rangemaster then locks the door, sealing us in.

"For your information, that wasn't a mass grave you stumbled upon tonight," Dr. Weize tells us. "I'm curious to hear what you think you know, but there was no need for us to speak about such matters in front of the help."

"I know that this was once a lab," I say. "I recognize that door as the type used in cleanrooms from my research for *Scientific Spinster*."

"I admit it…I'm impressed," Dr. Weize replies. "That door, as well as this room, also happens to be soundproof, so there's no point in yelling for help."

"If we was gonna do any yelling," Slim says, "we would've done it topside, you idget."

"Quite so." Dr. Weize approaches Slim and then slaps him across the face with the back of his hand. "Now hold your tongue, or I'll have the rangemaster cut it out and hold it for you. Let's return to your investigation, Mr. Payley. For my future reference, I want to know what you were able to discover; in return I'll sate your curiosity and tell you if you're right."

"I think somehow you knew there was to be a raid on your lab here," I say, "maybe you have someone from the sheriff's department on your payroll."

"No," Dr. Weize says, "but in retrospect that would've been a good idea. Before it became a lab, this space was in fact used as an underground shooting range just as the sheriff saw it when she executed her search warrant. When the lab was set up here, we had the shooting range equipment stored at the main house and a small radar system installed on the roof. I thought it an unnecessary precaution, but my benefactors insisted. Then when a low-flying aircraft flew over the exact location of the lab so soon after your visit to the Farm, I considered it too much of a coincidence and had the lab dismantled and the range set up again. My men had to work through the night to accomplish the task and finished just before the sheriff arrived in the morning. I even left behind my favorite Thompson submachine gun to make the subterfuge all the more convincing. I suspect you used some sort of infrared device to find this underground facility. With as many people down here as you must've seen when you flew overhead of what you were later led to believe was an active shooting range, I find it surprising that it didn't occur to you that there were no heat signatures from guns being fired. At any rate, I had the lab equipment, which included small tanks of methane used to fuel Bunsen burners, taken away in a cargo van and then buried near that oak tree the following night. One of the tanks must've ruptured when it was tossed into the hole, and that's why your partner got a reading on the methane detector he was using in the video I saw."

"So who are those goons in the ski masks?" I ask. "They don't strike me as guards from the Farm."

"No," Dr. Weize answers, "they're club members who are either ex-military or would-be paramilitary types that we keep on retainer and who reside full time at the main house."

"Is Geoff mixed up in all this?" I ask.

"Geoff," Dr. Weize replies with amusement, "no, he's just an idiot from old money—completely oblivious to this operation, as are most of our club members. We did have several members from the medical field who ran the lab, though thanks to you, that work is now done off-site."

"So if the remnants of the lab are buried where your thugs caught us, then where are the missing patients buried?" I ask.

"They're not buried," answers Dr. Weize.

"Then they really are missing?" I ask.

"In the sense that no one will ever find them...yes. Those unfortunate souls were some of our first test subjects who sadly experienced severe side effects to an early version of what was being developed in this lab. I had their bodies incinerated, using the fuel from some of the tanks you discovered tonight, so while you didn't find their bodies, you can take solace in the fact that you happened upon the means of their disposal. But enough of what you don't know, tell me what you do know...at least to the limit of your understanding."

"I may not have all the details worked out, like what was in those canisters you received yesterday, but the broad strokes are that you're running a slave plantation and lacing your so-called vitamins with a compound that you manufacture from corn that mimics an opioid but also disguises its effects, which—exacerbated by a severe corn allergy—is what killed the McCormick boy. Those capsules, which are benign until activated by iron in the well water your patients drink, keep the Big Farm inmates docile as well as keep them from overcoming their addictions, making them your willing slaves who you pay almost nothing and who will work for you almost indefinitely, all while getting rich yourself, which you enjoy, and being exalted for your work, which you enjoy even more. You've succeeded in restoring your reputation, which was blemished years ago, as an addiction specialist who has created an innovative treatment technique. I imagine to someone with your ego that failure really rankled you; however, all you've actually accomplished is keeping a bunch of addicts addicted, which doesn't seem like such an exceptional undertaking to me."

"I agree," Dr. Weize replies, "what you describe isn't exceptional at all. However, that's not what's underway here, though that bit about the iron in the well water functioning as an activating agent is quite ingenious—completely fictive, but ingenious nonetheless. No, the compound you mentioned builds up and is stored in the body's fat and then released slowly, like an IV drip, as that fat is converted into fuel, typically in the engagement of arduous labor, which induces our inmates to toil ever more intensely at their farmhand chores. I commend you for getting more of that right than I thought you would...even so, you still got most of it wrong, but then what can one expect from an author who writes such drivel as *Sleuthing Spinster*?"

"That's my bestselling book," I protest.

"And you call into question the motivation for my work," Dr. Weize continues. "I've gathered from our conversations that you enjoy wordplay, so you might be amused to know that the origin of the moniker Big Farm has nothing to do with agriculture. It comes from the genesis of this operation, which began when a large pharmaceutical corporation was beset by a class-action lawsuit concerning the synthetic opioids it manufactured. The drugs were created to combat chronic pain but regrettably resulted in addiction for many of the patients who were prescribed those opioids. Sensing an opportunity in the midst of the opioid crisis that our country is currently besieged by, this big pharm corporation began research into drugs to combat addiction but came to the same lamentable conclusion that I did all those years ago in my private practice: there's no cure for addiction. Once an addict, always an addict…the best that can be hoped for is to suppress the addictive tendencies. With that in mind, they contacted me in part due to the research my mentor and I had done early in my career, and yes, there is some truth to your assertion that all this has afforded me the opportunity to vindicate the treatment program that we developed, which could've worked if not for the meddling of our squeamish sponsors."

"So this big pharm corporation is developing drugs to suppress addiction, which is cute by the way— attempting to turn a profit from a problem it created, but then why did Sloan die of an overdose?"

"Once again, you've jumped to a conclusion based on an incomplete understanding of the facts. The McCormick boy was of particular interest to us precisely because of his severe corn allergy. We could tell from the chemical marker that showed up in his urine analysis that he was taking more than one dose of the vitamin a day, but despite being corn based, we'd calculated that we had refined the content of the capsules enough so as not to aggravate his allergies. What we did not anticipate was that the McCormick boy would be out in our test cornfield just after it had been sprayed with a designer fertilizer, which is what we have shipped to us in those canisters you mentioned—along with its counterpart, a proprietary hybrid seed corn. As some of the residue from the fertilizer began evaporating in that very hot field, the chemicals were inhaled by the boy, creating a toxic cocktail with the chemicals already in his system, and unfortunately he perished. Though I can assure you that the boy's sacrifice will pale in comparison to the good we intend to accomplish."

"It's only a sacrifice when you know you're making it," I say. "What happened to Sloan was murder."

"Your compassion is touching," replies Dr. Weize, "and if it's of any comfort, you'll soon be making the same sacrifice."

I choose to ignore the professor's ominous last remark. "We're in the middle of corn country. Why are you having special fertilizer and seed corn in unmarked canisters flown in on private planes when you could simply order anything you want from the local farm supply store?"

"Almost anything, but not quite everything," Dr. Weize corrects. "That's the part of our operation you've missed entirely. Corn is a very versatile grain, which is why it's found in so many different types of products; its global production surpasses that of wheat and rice. The mutability of corn allows it to be hybridized in phenomenal ways. During their R & D for a drug to cure addiction, this big pharm corporation came across work done at the Maize Genetics Center at my university, which incidentally is how I first came to their attention. They were able to co-opt some preliminary research for creating an opioid-like compound, which had been abandoned by the Center. Then the corporation acquired an agrochemical biotechnology company to create a designer fertilizer that would stimulate our hybrid corn to grow with those properties, which was then cultivated and processed in the lab here. I don't pretend to understand all the exotic chemistry behind it; suffice it to say that the compound under development doesn't cure addiction exactly but rather ameliorates its symptoms."

"I don't understand why this big pharm corporation would go to all the trouble to develop and test this sub-rosa cure, if it isn't really a cure. I doubt they could successfully bring a drug to market to combat addiction that from what you've explained doesn't really end the addiction but instead alters it."

"I doubt they could as well," Dr. Weize agrees, "and more importantly they doubt it too, but once again you've missed the grander picture. I told you once before that the opiate of the masses is opioids. The compounds created by the corn we grow work best on addicts whose brain chemistry has already been altered by opioids, but it should also work to forestall future addicts who are predisposed to addiction but who have not yet been exposed to opioids. Big Pharm is working on a formula for a fertilizer that will grow corn that doesn't require post-harvest processing, but rather will be processed in the body's digestive system, either as a direct consumer of the corn itself and foodstuffs created from it or as a consumer of animals that have eaten the corn. Their prediction is that they're within five years of a breakthrough."

"But you risk making addicts of us all."

"Of a sort," Dr. Weize confirms. "But that's the beauty of corn; it's eaten by all of us in some fashion almost every day. The ultimate goal is to flood the food supply with our corn—like fluoride in the water supply."

"Then what happens to someone who becomes…I don't know, a fruitarian after years of eating your corn?" I ask. "I know a former patient of yours who looks to be suffering from withdrawal right now."

"Yes, the potential for withdrawal symptoms following an abrupt cessation is one issue that has yet to be resolved," Dr. Weize admits. "Another is the compound testing positive as an opioid in a toxicology test after long-term exposure, but we've made enormous advances in a relatively short time, unfettered as we are in our covert trials from restrictive regulatory organizations and litigious nanny-state entities, so I'm confident that we'll solve both issues in due time. Besides, these things have a tendency to sort themselves out. I don't think we'll need to be too concerned with our consumers becoming fruitarians once they're addicted to the products that contain our compound. As for the testing issue, poppy seeds are consumed despite their potential to yield a positive result in a drug screening."

"So how do your benefactors intend to monetize their product if their plan is to just dump it into the food supply?" I ask. "I assume their ultimate goal is to make an unseemly amount of money, so they can't just give it away, and they can't market a product—no matter the perceived benefits—that results in a different sort of addiction."

"There are other ancillary benefits to our compound. While it doesn't have the same euphoric effects as opioids, it does have a palliative effect that will mask many of the aches and pains of our daily lives. Imagine what could be accomplished in the coming generations by a population with fewer complaints. So yes, our product will be free...for a time, but like every drug peddler on the street corner knows, it's good business to offer free samples, because the real money is made not by first-time users but by repeat customers. I told you before that the human mind isn't wired for happiness, but it is set up for addiction. If a consumer tries a box of cereal made from our corn and likes it better than his regular cereal, without fully understanding why, he'll make a change. If enough consumers make the same change, the old cereal maker will examine what's different about this new competing product and discover that it's made from our corn, so again, without fully understanding why, they'll make a change too, and so on. Within a decade or so, our corn—grown with our fertilizer—will have cornered the market, all without anyone but us fully understanding why."

"Eliminating free will along the way," I say.

"I would argue that an addict is predisposed to servitude, either to the illicit drugs that will eventually kill him and destroy society or to our product that will save him and make him a productive member of society. The one thing I've learned from all my years of working with addicts is that no one is above addiction."

"I didn't see it until this very moment," I say, "but you're completely insane—a psychology professor afflicted with extreme psychosis."

"The Nietzchean superman is not bound by law or morality," Dr. Weize retorts, "but rather by the ken of his privileged vision. I suspect in your narrow, simplistic view I must seem like a villain from one of your paltry stories, though now I suppose I understand why the villains inevitably reveal their master plans to the hero—like the stakes in that wager of ours when we shot skeet above where we're standing now: the chance for confession…and who better to confess to than someone who won't be around long enough to share your secrets?"

"Take it from an author who's written a lot of villains. Villainy is more about motive than objective, and if your goals really were altruistic, you'd be doing all this above board. And that's another thing, Mr. Man of Steel…what's with all the 'we' talk when it comes to this master plan? You outlined a grand vision indeed, full of smart people doing really twisted things—just awful stuff that I can't even imagine how they came up with in the first place, let alone summoned the temerity to act on it, but your role in all this seems…well, kind of like a rodeo clown whose only job is to be a distraction."

Out of the corner of my eye, I see a smile grow on Slim's face. Dr. Weize, who is definitely not smiling, moves toward the rangemaster.

"I mean, your addiction treatment techniques are clearly bullshit, you don't have a clue about the chemistry that's involved with the fertilizer, or the corn, or the drugs, and I bet you know even less about the actual goings-on higher up the ladder in the boardrooms where the real decisions are being made. It seems to me that the real reason you were chosen for this unsavory project is because you failed all those years ago, and instead of learning from that failure like a well-adjusted adult would, you went around bemoaning your failings like an ill-mannered child. You're not an architect of any exceptional undertaking or even its facilitator. If this were a horror movie, you wouldn't be Dr. Frankenstein or the Monster...you'd merely be Igor, the moronic assistant who's as clumsy as he is useless—comic relief at best."

Dr. Weize, who has the rangemaster's hand cannon now, walks toward me and raises the gun to my forehead.

"You question my role in all this." Dr. Weize presses the firearm's muzzle against the front of my skull. "My job is to make sure things run efficiently and that people are kept quiet."

I'm glad I updated my will a few months ago to leave everything to Becca. "You know, Judy, despite being an ineffectual intellectual and just an all-around dipshit, the one thing I respect about you is that you're a man of your word—like what you said about our shooting wager; you made your bet, you lost, and you paid up."

Dr. Weize lowers the gun. "I sense that you're about to propose another wager."

"I am. You've spilled your naughty little secrets, so obviously you're going to kill me, but I could tell all along by the way you kept tipping your hand—as if daring me to figure out what you were up to—that you enjoy playing games. You're a sportsman, Dr. Weize, so then kill me in a sporting way. I suspect you're something of an oddity here at this club—a gun collector who's a vegetarian that doesn't hunt, so I suggest a duel. It'll give you a chance to test your mettle as a marksman, since I imagine it's more of a challenge to hit a target with a mind of its own, especially one that can shoot back at you. There's very little risk for you as I've never fired a handgun before, and the only time I've ever fired a gun at all was during our last contest. If you kill me, which is the most likely outcome, your reputation and this operation will remain intact, whereas if I kill you, none of this will be your concern any longer. Our circumstances have given you a unique opportunity that you may never get again. You and I are both old enough to know that we've got more years behind us than ahead; we only get one go around…why not make it interesting?"

Chapter 19

Dr. Weize stares at me with an unnerving smile as he silently considers my proposition. Then he returns the handgun to the rangemaster.

"I accept your proposal," Dr. Weize says, "and as it happens, I have a pair of dueling pistols down here that I recently had restored—Russian antiques purported to have been used in a duel involving Alexander Pushkin, which as a writer I'm sure you will appreciate."

"I'd appreciate it a lot more if they came with rubber bullets," I reply, "but let's get on with it, shall we?"

Dr. Weize retrieves an ornate wooden box from a tall gun safe against the wall while the rangemaster keeps watch over me and Slim.

"And I thought you talked a lot," Slim says quietly.

"He's a loquacious one all right," I reply. "So what sort of odds do you give me?"

"About the same as what you gave me earlier tonight, but if I were a betting man, my money would still be on you."

"Thanks, Slim...sorry I got you into all this. Maybe I should've taken your advice and just left this thing alone."

"Maybe, but you saw a wrong that needed setting right...that's something to be proud of."

"Pride goeth before destruction." Dr. Weize returns with the box, which he opens to reveal two handsomely crafted flintlock pistols. "As you can see, these exquisite pieces are identical, but since they belong to me, you may have first choice."

The rangemaster flicks open a pocketknife and cuts the zip tie holding my hands behind my back. I choose the pistol nearest to Dr. Weize. The wood and steel gun feels solid and has a nice heft. I grip the handle and look down the barrel.

"Good then," says Dr. Weize. "The rangemaster will be my second and act as a referee of sorts for these proceedings. Mr. Payley, your partner will be your second, though I must insist that his hands remain bound. The rangemaster will load your pistol for you."

"We can manage ourselves," Slim says.

"Very well," replies Dr. Weize.

The professor signals to the rangemaster, who then hands me a powder flask and a lead shot from the box.

"One last item," Dr. Weize says. "You mentioned that you found it odd that I've never hunted…and given my penchant for firearms, I suppose it is. In the spirit of taking full advantage of these unique circumstances, I stipulate that rather than the standard walk-ten-paces-and-turn type of duel that we instead have ourselves a hunt. I will give you a three-minute head start into the shooting gallery before I come find you. Agreed?"

"Sure," I say, "sounds like fun."

"I'm glad you think so." Dr. Weize flips several light switches on the wall near the gun safe. A series of overhead fluorescent lights come to life, revealing the true enormity of the room. The shooting range is reminiscent of a Hollywood set, with building façades and props made to look like a street corner in a post-apocalyptic city. "Before we begin, you may confer with your second for a moment as I do so with mine."

"I told you...gun nuts." Slim turns around and raises his hands as high as he can. "Give me your pistol and the powder flask." Despite not being able to see his hands, Slim adroitly pours black powder down the pistol's muzzle. "Now hand me the shot." I take back the powder flask and put the lead ball covered in cloth into Slim's free hand. He drops it into the muzzle and then pulls the ramrod out from under the barrel. He jams it down into the muzzle, tamping it a few times. Satisfied, he tosses the ramrod onto the floor and hands me the pistol. "At least we know the damn thing is loaded properly."

"Thanks...so should I aim for his head?"

"No, shoot for center mass."

"What do you mean...like around his belly button? I imagine he probably already has a hole there."

"You've just got one shot with that pistol, so only take the shot you know you can make."

Dr. Weize calls out from near the light switches, "Are you ready?"

"As I'll ever be," I answer.

"Excellent. Now that you've seen our shooting range, I'll turn out all the lights save those nearest the door, just as it was when you first arrived, giving you a chance to conceal yourself in the darkness. After three minutes, I'll turn on the slow strobe light, which will afford each of us windows of opportunity to move around in the shadows...or to get caught in the light. The rangemaster, who is equipped with night-vision goggles, will follow you out onto the shooting range to ensure that you don't try anything unsportsmanlike, such as using the black powder in your pistol to set the wooden props ablaze and burn us all alive or taking a potshot at me from the darkness before the three minutes are up. Otherwise, he has promised not to interfere. You said you know me to be a man of my word, so I give you my word that he is as well. Does that sound fair?"

"Fair enough," I say, "though you might've saved half the cost of the goggles if you'd equipped your one-eyed henchman with a night-vision monocle instead."

"I'm so pleased that you've retained your sense of humor." Dr. Weize flips the light switches again and plunges most of the room into darkness. "It'll make killing you all the more gratifying."

Slim gives me a nod. I walk out onto the shooting range. The rangemaster follows at a distance, giving me room to maneuver. I make my way along the building fronts, but by the time I reach the corner building, I need to grope around in the darkness to navigate. I hear the rangemaster's footsteps several yards behind me. I briefly consider shooting him and taking his gun that likely has a full clip, but I only have a general sense of where he is, while I'm sure he can see me plain as day. Hearing him reminds me of what Edwin has said before about how I sound when I walk, so I take off my shoes.

The strobe light comes on, and Dr. Weize shouts, "Ready or not."

I quickly duck into a doorway. A few moments later, from behind the building façade, I see Dr. Weize pass by an open window three buildings down, but before I can take aim, we are cast into shadow by the slowly pulsating light. I arrange my shoes just inside the doorway so that only the tips are visible from the outside at the angle of the professor's approach. I climb the lattice work of two-by-fours connecting the plywood façades up to the second level. Then I wait.

When the light comes back on, I see Dr. Weize below through the window whose sill I'm holding onto with my free hand, but my grip is loosening, and the two-by-four my toes are on doesn't offer much support. The professor nears the vicinity of the doorway. I raise my gun hand to my head and press my index finger against the side of my nose. I execute a stealthy farmer blow. The mucus projectile makes a barely audible noise when it lands on the concrete floor just past my shoes, but in the quiet room, it's enough to attract his attention.

Alerted to my presence, Dr. Weize espies the tips of my shoes and cautiously approaches the doorway. He sidles up to the edge of the entrance, and without fully entering, he thrusts his arm inside. Just as I let go my grip and push off of the two-by-four to land on his arm below, he pokes his head into the doorway and spots my true position. He raises his pistol up in my direction as I drop down to his. Then the lights go out.

All I see is a shower of sparks, followed quickly by a deafening bang. A fervent pain introduces itself when I land on the floor. I attempt to gather my wits as I lie in the darkness, but before I can move, I feel the professor's hands at my throat, trying to choke the life from me. I am no longer holding my pistol, so I reach out into the darkness. I can feel the gun's handle with my fingertips, but rather than stretch out for it, I bring both my hands to my attacker's face and plunge my thumbs into his eye sockets as I feel myself begin to black out.

Dr. Weize howls in agony and topples off me, releasing his stranglehold. The lights come back on, and I grab my pistol. As I attempt to regain my feet, I become aware that my left foot is a bloody mess. I brace myself against the back of the plywood façade and stand over Dr. Weize, who is cowering in the doorway and appears to be partially blinded. I limp toward the professor and put the muzzle of my pistol to his forehead. I notice the rangemaster standing nearby, his gun at his side. He gives me a nod, as if signaling me to deliver the coup de grâce.

I cock the pistol. "This is a shot I know I can make." Dr. Weize shuts his bleeding eyes. I quickly spin in the direction of the rangemaster and pull the trigger, shooting him in the shoulder. He drops his gun and crumples to the floor.

Dr. Weize opens his eyes. I raise my gun, which I'm now holding like a hammer, above the professor. "You just bought the farm." I pistol-whip the good doctor into unconsciousness.

I limp over to the rangemaster, who seems to be losing consciousness himself from blood loss, and take his gun and pocketknife. I make my way back toward Slim, who I now realize, after the ringing in my ears subsides, has been calling out for me, "Weston, you okay?"

"I'm a little injured." I continue in the direction of his voice. "But not so badly as the other two."

I discover that Dr. Weize had tied up Slim with rope to the now-locked gun safe. When he sees me limp out of the shadows, the look on his face is priceless. I cut him free with the knife and turn on the lights. Then he takes the rope and the handgun and goes back out into the shooting range to ensure that Dr. Weize and the rangemaster are still incapacitated.

Chapter 20

Slim returns sans rope after a few moments to find me slumped against the door. "They're both unconscious, though I tied them up just to be safe. You did good, but why'd you shoot the rangemaster instead of Judy?"

"I figured he'd keep his word about not interfering, but I also figured once the duel was over, he wasn't just going to let us walk out of here and expose their operation."

"I see your point, but we ain't exactly out of the woods yet. We still got those two goons with shotguns on the other side of this door, and even if it is soundproof, by now they're likely wondering what's going on in here. Not to mention the mess of militia that's probably topside, and we only got the one gun between us."

"I've got a knife."

Slim smiles. "I like your spirit, but you'd just be a limping target. Besides, you've done your share already."

I stand up as best I can. Slim shakes my hand. "It's been an honor."

"For me too," I reply.

"If you happen to make it out of this alive and I don't...promise me that you'll take my boy fishing."

"I promise to take him fishing all the time...when it's warm."

Slim raises his gun and readies himself. He takes a deep breath and throws open the door.

"Don't shoot," a familiar voice implores.

In a scene of complete incongruity, I see Geoff standing in the doorway with his hands in the air next to the woman with an afro from the Shady Tree who's holding a shotgun.

"Geoff?" I ask, mystified. "What the hell are you doing here?"

"It's rather a long story," he says, "but the short version is that we're attempting to effect your rescue."

I look to the lady for more explanation and notice the pair of now unmasked goons in handcuffs on the floor in the hallway with three uniformed deputies standing over them.

"I used to be a guard out at the Big Farm until I got on with the sheriff's department," she tells me. "I've had my suspicions about that place ever since those inmates went missing, and when you turned up last night asking questions, I thought maybe you were onto something. I knew Dr. Weize was a member of this club, so I came out here with the sheriff to ask him some questions, which is when we met your friend. He said he knew you and had happened to see a cargo van that looked out of place driving around on the property, so we came out here to check on things."

"We're damn glad you did," Slim says, looking slightly less perplexed than I feel.

"The sheriff and some other deputies are out rounding up the rest of these militia morons," Geoff adds. "I always thought those odious individuals didn't meet the standards for membership of this club."

"Enough with the gum flapping and back patting," Slim says. "We need to get this man to the hospital to have his foot tended to."

"I quite agree." Geoff moves out of the doorway and offers absolutely no assistance whatsoever.

Slim puts my arm over his shoulder, and we hobble down the hallway. I can hear Geoff behind me with the female deputy.

"They'll be sorting out this business for hours yet. How about you and I go have an early breakfast together?"

"You buying?" the lady asks.

"Hell yes, I'm rich."

Chapter 21

I see a blurry figure standing over me as I struggle to open my eyes...a blurry figure with a huge, round belly.

"Easy," Becca says, "you're coming out of the anesthesia."

"It's really good to see you." I look around the room and things start to come into focus. "How did the operation go?"

"Mostly good."

"Mostly good...what part went bad?"

"The surgeon said you'll be able to walk normally in no time and that you should be able to leave the hospital tomorrow, but she wasn't able to save all your toes."

"How many did I lose?" I try to sit up to look at my bandaged left foot.

"Just one...the little one."

"But that's the one that goes 'wee, wee, wee' all the way home."

Slim peeks through the narrow window in the door, and seeing that I'm awake, he enters the room.

"How are you feeling, partner?"

"As soon as I regrow my missing toe, I'll be fine."

"You got nine more," Slim reminds me. "Quit your bellyaching."

"Did they get Dr. Weize to talk?" I ask.

"Some," Slim answers. "He's confessed to his role, but he's yet to divulge the names of his employers, though I'm confident he'll cooperate eventually. He's just down the hall under armed guard, recovering from a skull fracture...poor fella. I thought I'd drop in on him later and say howdy."

"Did you hear me when I told him 'you just bought the farm'?"

Slim rubs the back of his neck. "Yeah, I thought I heard you say something like that."

"Pretty good tough-guy repartee, huh?"

"Well, it didn't really make sense to me. I mean he worked out at the Big Farm, but it's not like he was going to buy it or anything, and it wasn't like you were really trying to kill him either."

"Right...I guess maybe it sounded like a better line in the heat of the moment."

"But that was a great shot you got off at the rangemaster," Slim is quick to add. "That old boy's still in surgery."

"Thanks, I'm thinking of entitling my next book *Sharpshooting Spinster*."

"Just do me a favor...don't write me as some yokel cop who all he does is drink beer and talk about fishing."

"It's a deal," I fib.

"Speaking of fishing, when you get out of here, we'll have to take another crack at ice fishing."

"Please don't use the word 'crack' when you talk about ice fishing with me. The only winter fishing I plan to do from now on will be when I'm vacationing someplace warm...if that."

"The ice would be good for numbing the pain in your foot," Slim says.

"But it won't do much for the pain in my ass from sitting on that damn bucket. But seriously, Slim...ice fishing sucks."

"Fine, we'll go drinking instead, and I'll let you buy the beer."

"That hardly seems fair...I'm the amputee after all."

"Okay, boys," Becca says, "you two can figure it out later, but right now my guy needs some sleep."

"All right then." Slim turns to leave. "You rest up. I'll be back to check on you later."

As he exits the room, I say, "I thought he'd never leave." I see Slim's grin through the narrow window.

"You two certainly seem to be getting on well," Becca teases.

"I only have eyes for you, and these days I need to keep them both wide open if I want to see all of you at once."

She looks at the spare pillow on my bed like she's considering using it to smother me. "Mayor McCormick stopped by while you were still unconscious. He said they tested all the patients at the Big Farm, and as you predicted, Gus was one of the few whose test didn't come back positive. Given these 'extraordinary circumstances' as the mayor put it, he thinks Rod...Rodney will be cleared of his parole violation and placed in a new treatment program along with all the other patients."

"How's Rodney doing?" I ask.

"He was exhibiting pretty severe withdrawal symptoms, so they've got him on methadone for now.

He'll need to restart his drug therapy all over again, but at least he's not going to prison."

"That's good…I hope the boys get a chance to see him soon."

"Me too."

"How did the mayor seem to you?"

"Sanguine. He intends to push for the Big Farm to be converted into a juvenile addiction-treatment facility. He wants to have it named the Sloan McCormick Farm."

"I like the sound of that."

"So do I." Becca leans over and kisses my forehead. "Get some sleep now. I'm going to do the same right over there in that recliner."

I hand her my spare pillow, trusting that she'll only use it for its intended purpose, and then close my eyes. Sleep comes easily.

Chapter 22

One final bit of business. The doctor gave me a pair of crutches and the all clear to go home. Becca carries my bag as we make our way out of the hospital to my car in the parking lot.

"I'll drive," I say.

"Are you sure?"

"Absolutely…I only need my right foot to drive. Besides, I feel uncomfortable when I'm in my own car and someone else is driving."

"Yeah, Vancy mentioned that."

"He did?" I toss the crutches onto the backseat and then gingerly get into the driver's seat.

I pull out of the parking lot and onto the busy street. It's a sunny day, and I'm glad to be out of the hospital, but I don't feel in a particular hurry to go anyplace. I drive at a leisurely pace as cars pass us on the left.

"Early for church, Grandma?" Becca asks.

I begin to make a brilliant bon mot but then notice up ahead at the railroad tracks that the warning lights of the crossing gate have started to flash.

"Not this time." I floor the accelerator. "If my brush with death taught me anything, it's that life's too short for idle waiting."

"Firstly, I'm not sure losing a toe qualifies as a brush with death. Secondly, if we get hit by a train, our lives are going to be very short indeed. Thirdly, you won't make it."

"Don't worry, I'm not going to put you or the baby in any danger." I catch up to the car in front of us, which is also trying to beat the descending gate. "If the arm comes down, I won't go around." The vehicle ahead clears the tracks. I speed up and see the gate in my rearview mirror just miss hitting the trunk lid. "See…plenty of time." We bounce over the bumpy tracks. "I just spent the last couple of days confined to a bed, so I don't intend to spend any more time at a standstill."

Becca looks at me with an anxious expression as we drive past the line of cars waiting to go in the opposite direction. "My water just broke."

"Should we go back to the hospital?"

"Unless you want me to have the baby in your car."

"That wouldn't be optimal." I drive to the end of the stalled convoy and execute a U-turn, taking our place as the last car in line. "I loathe waiting for trains." I shift my car into park. "I'm sure it must be an indicator of some sort of character flaw, but I don't have the patience to suss it out."

"You're annoyed that we're stuck here?" Becca's breathing gets all weird. "I'm the one going into labor!"

"I know how you feel. I did just lose an appendage after all, but tell me—are you familiar with the nobility of suffering in silence?"

"Do you really think that losing one little toe hurts worse than childbirth?"

"Apparently it must, since I'd do just about anything not to lose a second toe, but you seem to be in a hurry to give birth for the third time."

"You are infuriating!"

"I know, my dear, but it's only because I'm attempting to keep your mind off the discomfort."

And so it goes.

A word about the author...

Wesley Payton has a B.A. in Rhetoric/Philosophy and an M.A. in English. He has been a short-story presenter for the Illinois Philological Association. His play *Way Station* was selected for a Next Draft reading in 2015, and *What Does a Question Weigh?* was selected for a staged reading as part of the 2017 Chicago New Work Festival. He is the author of the novels *Lead Tears, Darkling Spinster, Darkling Spinster No More, Standing in Doorways*, and *Raison Deidre*. Wes and his family live in Oak Park, Illinois.

Weston Payley will appear next in *The House Painter and the Pirate Hunter* and then return in *Immurdered: Some Time to Kill*.

Find out more about Wesley and his books here:
http://wespayton.weebly.com/